THE CHILD'S WORLD®

ENCYCLOPEDIA
of BASEBALL

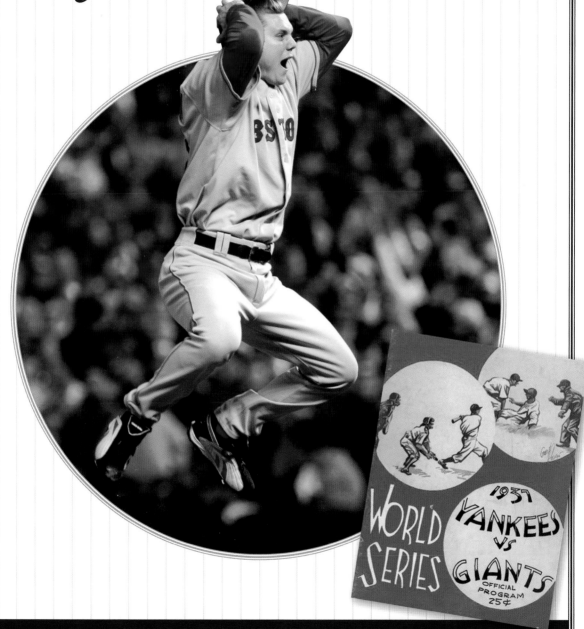

VOLUME 5: TAG THROUGH BARRY ZITO

By James Buckley, Jr., David Fischer, Jim Gigliotti, and Ted Keith

KEY TO SYMBOLS

Throughout *The Child's World® Encyclopedia of Baseball*, you'll see these symbols.
They'll give you a quick clue pointing to each entry's general subject area.

Active player | **Baseball word or phrase** | **Hall of Fame** | **Miscellaneous** | **Ballpark** | **Team**

The Child's World
www.childsworld.com

Published in the United States of America by The Child's World®
1980 Lookout Drive, Mankato, MN 56003-1705
800-599-READ • www.childsworld.com

ACKNOWLEDGMENTS

The Child's World®: Mary Berendes, Publishing Director

Produced by Shoreline Publishing Group LLC
President / Editorial Director: James Buckley, Jr.
Cover Design: Kathleen Petelinsek, The Design Lab
Interior Design: Tom Carling, carlingdesign.com
Assistant Editors: Jim Gigliotti, Zach Spear

Cover Photo Credits: AP/Wide World (main); National Baseball Hall of Fame Library (inset)
Interior Photo Credits: AP/Wide World: 9, 10, 15, 16, 20, 21, 24, 28, 35, 36, 37, 40, 43, 48, 51, 54, 56, 57, 60, 61, 62, 64, 65, 66, 68, 69, 70, 71, 76, 79; Corbis: 77; Dreamstime.com: Scott Downs 8; Focus on Baseball: 4, 6, 7, 11, 12, 13, 14, 17, 18, 19, 23, 29, 31, 73, 75; National Baseball Hall of Fame Library: 25, 26, 27, 30, 32, 33, 34, 39, 42, 44, 49, 52, 53, 72, 78; Rucker Archive: 5

LIBRARY OF CONGRESS CATALOG-IN-PUBLICATION DATA

The Child's World encyclopedia of baseball / by James Buckley, Jr. ... [et al.].
    p. cm. – (The Child's World encyclopedia of baseball)
  Includes index.
  ISBN 978-1-60253-167-3 (library bound : alk. paper)–ISBN 978-1-60253-168-0 (library bound : alk. paper)–ISBN 978-1-60253-169-7 (library bound : alk. paper)–ISBN 978-1-60253-170-3 (library bound : alk. paper)–ISBN 978-1-60253-171-0 (library bound : alk. paper)
  1. Baseball–United States–Encyclopedias, Juvenile. I. Buckley, James, 1963- II. Child's World (Firm) III. Title. IV. Series.

GV867.5.C46 2009
796.3570973–dc22

2008039461

R0422845454

Red Sox great Ted Williams.

PEOPLE HAVE BEEN PLAYING BASEBALL, America's national, pastime, for more than 150 years, so we needed a lot of room to do it justice! The five big volumes of *The Child's World˙ Encyclopedia of Baseball* hold as much as we could squeeze in about this favorite sport.

The Babe. The Say-Hey Kid. The Iron Horse. The Splendid Splinter. Rapid Robert. Hammerin' Hank. You'll read all about these great players of yesterday. You'll also learn about your favorite stars of today: Pujols, Jeter, Griffey, Soriano, Santana, Manny, and Big Papi. How about revisiting some of baseball's most memorable plays and games?

The Shot Heard 'Round the World. The Catch. The Grand-Slam Single. You'll find all of these–and more.

Have a favorite big-league team? They're all here, with a complete history for each team that includes its all-time record.

Ever wonder what it means to catch a can of corn, hit a dinger, or use a fungo? Full coverage of baseball's unique and colorful terms will let you understand and speak the language as if you were born to it.

This homegrown sport is a part of every child's world, and our brand-new encyclopedia makes reading about it almost as fun as playing it!

Meet the Washington Nationals.

Contents: Volume 5: Tag ›› Barry Zito

■ *You're out! A fielder slaps a tag onto a sliding runner.*

Tag

A fielder makes a tag by touching a baserunner with the ball or by touching him with a glove holding the ball. A tag can also be made when in possession of the ball by touching a base with any part of the body if the runner is forced to go to that base. If a player is tagged when not in contact with a base, he is called out.

It's less common, but "tag" also can mean to hit the ball a long way: "He really tagged that one!"

Tag Up

Runners can advance to the next base on a ball that is caught in the air only if they touch the base they already are on *after* the catch is made. That is, they "tag up" after the catch.

Tagging up can occur on any fly ball or line drive with fewer than two outs, but it most often happens when there's a long fly ball with a runner on third base. The runner will retreat to the bag and wait for the catch to be made. Once the ball hits the fielder's glove, the runner races for home plate.

If the runner leaves the base before the ball is caught, the fielding team can record another out by touching that base with the ball in possession before another pitch is made.

Take

To "take" a pitch means to let it go by without swinging at it. It's almost always a batter's decision when he takes a pitch, although managers sometimes give him a take sign on a 3 and 0 count. They choose this play to try to create walks. When poor-hitting pitchers are at the plate, too, they might be given a take sign on any count with fewer than two strikes.

An old baseball axiom says that hitters on a losing team late in a game and in need of baserunners take a strike before trying to get a hit. That is, they try to draw a walk or turn the count in their favor instead of making an out on a bad pitch.

"Take Me Out to the Ball Game"

"Take Me Out to the Ball Game" is the song traditionally sung during the seventh-inning stretch–the period after the visiting team has hit in the top of the seventh and before the home team comes to bat–of a baseball game. The version almost always heard (see below) is actually only the chorus of a song originally written in 1908 by Jack Norworth and set to music by Albert Von Tilzer–neither of whom had ever been to a baseball game at the time.

In the 1970s, Chicago White Sox broadcaster Harry Caray began taking the public-address microphone in the middle of the seventh inning of home games and singing "Take Me Out to the Ball Game" to the crowd in his unique style. Caray continued to do so after moving across town to do Cubs' games beginning in 1982. Since Caray's death in 1997, various celebrities have kept up the tradition by taking their turns singing the song at Wrigley Field.

Here are the lyrics to the chorus (see the full song on page 80):

Take me out to the ball game,
Take me out with the crowd;
Buy me some peanuts and cracker jack,
I don't care if I never get back.
Let me root, root, root for the home team,
If they don't win, it's a shame.
For it's one, two, three strikes, you're out,
At the old ball game.

Tampa Bay Rays

Please see pages 6–7.

T-Ball

T-Ball, which is sometimes spelled "tee-ball," is a version of baseball most often played by very young kids who are just starting out in the sport. It gets its name from a stationary tee placed at home plate. Batters hit a ball placed on that tee instead of facing live pitching.

The game is usually played on a small diamond and with any number of players in the field. Sometimes, outs and runs are

continued on page 8

■ *The original music for the famous song.*

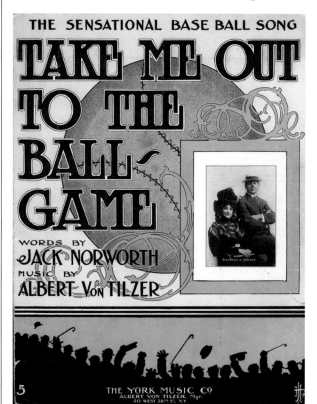

Tampa Bay Rays

In 2008, the Tampa Bay Rays got a new name (they used to be called the Tampa Bay Devil Rays), new uniforms—and a whole new attitude. For the first time in its 11-year history, Tampa Bay no longer played the role of the punching bag in the

■ *Crawford is an exciting, all-around player.*

traditionally strong American League Eastern Division. Instead, the Rays were the team that was beating up on opponents. They led the division most of the season, and finished the year with 97 wins and only 65 losses. That was good enough to finish one game ahead of Boston, the defending World Series champion, in the East and to clinch the first playoff appearance in club history.

Until 2008, the Rays' best season was in 2004, when they won a club-record 70 games. Manager Lou Piniella guided the team out of the five-team A.L. East's cellar for the first time in club history that year, but the team still finished 30.5 games behind the champion New York Yankees.

The Rays' history began as an expansion team in 1998—although the history of baseball in South Florida goes back a lot farther than that. Florida, of course, has been the spring-training home for many years for teams that play in the "Grapefruit League" the collective nickname given to the big-league teams that play in the Sunshine State each March. In 1922, the Boston Braves were the first team to begin training in Florida in the spring, and other Major League clubs soon followed suit.

The strong interest in Major League Baseball in Florida made it natural to consider placing a team in Tampa for the regular season, not just the spring. At different times, several teams looked as if they might relocate there. First, it was the Chicago White Sox in the late 1980s. Then it was the Seattle Mariners. Then it was the San Francisco Giants. But all of those teams eventually got new ballparks built and stayed in their cities.

Finally, in 1998, Tampa began play as an expansion team in the American League. The club got its original nickname from entries submitted in a newspaper contest. A devil ray is a type of manta ray, which is a large underwater creature. Picture something that looks like a swimming bat—the flying kind, not the baseball kind!

The first Rays' team won only 63 games, but it did have some notable players, including future Hall of Famer Wade Boggs. He was a Tampa native who hit the first home run in club history. Roland Arrojo's 14 wins marked the most ever by a pitcher for an expansion team. And outfielder Quinton McCracken's 179 hits were another expansion team record.

The next year, Boggs joined baseball's prestigious 3,000-hit club, and veteran first baseman Fred McGriff hit 32 home runs and drove in 104 runs. Still, Tampa won only 69 games.

The last-place finishes continued, except for the lone fourth-place finish in 2004. That year was significant, too, because 20-year-old left-hander Scott Kazmir made his big-league debut in August. Kazmir would soon develop into one of the best young starting pitchers in baseball.

■ *Evan Longoria, a top third baseman.*

Another Tampa Bay star is outfielder Carl Crawford. He is a classic "five-tool" player—a man who can hit for average, hit for power, and run, field, and throw well. Crawford led the American League in stolen bases four times in his first five seasons beginning in 2003 and made the All-Star Game twice.

Kazmir, Crawford, pitcher James Shields, and third baseman Evan Longoria—the American League's Rookie of the Year—helped fuel manager Joe Maddon's surprising club in 2008. The Rays won the A.L. title, but lost to the Phillies in the World Series.

TAMPA BAY RAYS

LEAGUE: **AMERICAN**

DIVISION: **EAST**

YEAR FOUNDED: **1998**

CURRENT COLORS:
BLACK, PURPLE, AND GREEN

STADIUM (CAPACITY):
TROPICANA FIELD (45,000)

ALL-TIME RECORD (THROUGH 2008):
742–1,037

WORLD SERIES TITLES:
NONE

not even counted. Rather, T-ball is just a way of introducing children to the concepts of batting, running, and fielding.

Teams in the field often have adults with them to help learn the right positions to play. In some leagues, older children do this job to help them learn to coach.

President George W. Bush, who used to be an owner of the Texas Rangers, made T-ball a part of his presidency. On 20 different occasions, he hosted children's T-ball games on the South Lawn of the White House. Dozens of kids got the chance to play ball at the president's home.

Major League players also use tees to practice their hitting into a net.

■ *T-ball is a great way to start playing baseball.*

Television, Baseball and

On August 26, 1939, the Dodgers and the Cincinnati Reds played a double-header at Brooklyn's Ebbets Field. They split the twin bill, with the visiting Reds winning the first game 5–2 and the host Dodgers taking the second 6–1. More importantly, however, those were the first two Major League Baseball games ever televised. Legendary announcer Red Barber called the action.

Today, most Major League games are on over-the-air, cable, or satellite television in at least one of the competing teams' markets. All games are available throughout the country for viewing on the Internet via a premium service offered by MLB.com.

Like all major pro sports, baseball was a beneficiary of the televised sports boom of the 1950s. By late in the decade, most American households had televisions. And for the first time, people who could not get out to a Major League game could see their heroes in live action.

Baseball, however, did not reap quite the benefits that sports such as pro football did. Football action fit the rectangular television screen perfectly, and its starts and stops worked well with the format. Baseball's diamond and its relaxing pace were not as perfect a fit. In addition, baseball fans had long identified with their teams and stars through games broadcast on the radio. Television, too, is sometimes blamed for the decline of many minor leagues and independent leagues. That's because people were able to stay home and see big-league stars on TV instead of going out to the park.

Still, television offered Major League Baseball greater exposure, as well as

■ *TV cameras and reporters swarm star players.*

additional money. Before TV, game tickets were the main source of money for teams. Today, huge contracts with television networks are shared by all teams; each individual club can make local deals, too.

In 1947, a World Series game was televised for the first time—only in New York, though, where most of America's television sets were located. Three years later, the All-Star Game was on TV. And one year after that, WCBS-TV in New York televised a game in color for the first time. Bobby Thomson's pennant-clinching home run for the New York Giants against the Brooklyn Dodgers in a 1951 playoff came in the first game televised coast-to-coast. NBC showed it.

In 1953, television began airing a baseball "Game of the Week" on Saturdays—a tra-

dition that continues to this day. ABC originated the idea, although only a few teams were involved at first. CBS took over the series a couple of years later, then it because a network staple at NBC from the late 1960s through the 1980s. Today, the Fox Network shows the Game of the Week.

In November of 2006, Major League owners unanimously approved television contracts with Fox and TBS that run through the 2013 season. The deal called for Fox to continue televising its Saturday afternoon regular-season games, as well as the All-Star Game and the World Series. TBS got the Division Series of the playoffs, while the two networks agreed to share the Championship Series. They've come a long way—the total of the deal was worth $3 billion.

Texas Rangers

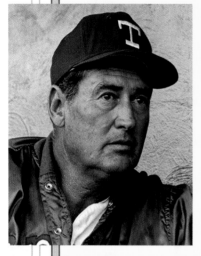

■ *Ted Williams managed the Rangers.*

The Texas Rangers have a colorful history that dates to 1961, when the franchise began play as the Washington Senators. Hall of Famers such as Ted Williams and Nolan Ryan, and big-name stars like Frank Howard, Juan Gonzalez, and Alex Rodriguez—plus even an owner named George W. Bush—all are part of the club's history. Unfortunately, whether in Washington or in Texas, the club has not been able to turn that kind of star power into victories on the field.

Washington, D.C., had been home to the Senators of the A.L. from 1901 until 1961. The Senators moved to the Minneapolis-St. Paul area, and they became the Minnesota Twins.

A new Senators' team took their place in Washington that same year. An expansion team, that club had no more success than the previous version of the Senators—neither on the field nor at the gate. So even though burly slugger Frank Howard was belting mammoth home-run blasts, and all-time great outfielder Ted Williams tried his hand at managing the team, the Senators generally found themselves mired in the bottom half of the standings. In 1972, Washington lost another Senators' team when the club relocated to Arlington, Texas, and became the Rangers.

The early Rangers' teams featured some good players, like outfielder Jeff Burroughs, the American League's MVP for 1974. He hit .301 and drove in 118 runs as the Rangers finished in second place that year in the A.L. West. It was their best season yet.

For much of the next two decades, though, the Rangers only occasionally had good teams. In 1990, fireballing right-hander Nolan Ryan, baseball's all-time strikeout king, joined the club. The native Texan and future Hall of Famer notched his 300th career victory at age 43 that year. He also pitched his record sixth and seventh career no-hitters while in a Texas uniform. Ryan retired at 46 in 1993.

TEXAS RANGERS

LEAGUE: **AMERICAN**

DIVISION: **WEST**

YEAR FOUNDED: **1961**

CURRENT COLORS:
RED AND BLUE

STADIUM (CAPACITY):
RANGERS BALLPARK IN ARLINGTON (48,911)

ALL-TIME RECORD
(THROUGH 2008):
3,570–4,059

WORLD SERIES TITLES:
NONE

By then, George W. Bush, who would become President of the United States in 2000, owned the team. He was part of an ownership group that took over in 1989.

Little changed in the won-lost column for Texas, however, until 1996. Outfielder Juan Gonzalez was the star, earning league MVP honors that year while hitting .314 with 47 homers and 144 RBI for the first squad in franchise history to make the playoffs. Texas went 90–72 under manager Johnny Oates and won the American League West.

That began a string of three division championships in four years. In 1998, Gonzalez won his second MVP award—he hit .318 this time with 45 homers and 157 RBI—and the Rangers won 88 games and another division title. The next year, it was a club-record 95 wins and the A.L. West crown. Right-hander Aaron Sele was the pitching star that year, winning a career-best 19 games and earning an All-Star selection.

Each of the Rangers' three division championships, though, ended in disappointing first-round losses in playoff series against the powerful New York Yankees. Texas hasn't been back to the playoffs since. In fact, in that time, they've had only one winning season: 89–73 in 2004.

It hasn't been for lack of star power, however. In 2001, the Rangers signed former Seattle Mariners shortstop Alex Rodriguez to

■ *Josh Hamilton is the latest Texas slugger.*

a 10-year, $252-million contract—the largest in pro sports history. He put up amazing numbers in three seasons in Texas, even winning A.L. MVP honors in 2003. But his big contract left little money for signing other good players, and he eventually was traded to the Yankees in 2004.

The lastest big slugger for Texas is Josh Hamilton, who led the American League with 130 RBI 2008.

Tejada, Miguel

Four-time All-Star Miguel Tejada is a power-hitting shortstop for the Houston Astros and a former American League MVP. Tejada was just 19 years old when the Oakland A's signed him out of the Dominican Republic in 1993. (Oakland thought he was 17 at the time—stay tuned

■ *Tejada once played 1,105 games in a row.*

for more on that!). Tejada broke into the Majors in 1997 and hit 21 home runs as a full-time starter for the first time in 1999. He hit 30 homers the next year, marking the first of three seasons in a row that he reached that mark. In 2002, he hit .308 with 131 RBI to go along with his 34 home runs. Those numbers earned him league MVP honors.

Two years later, Tejada signed a free-agent contract with the Baltimore Orioles and belted 34 homers while driving in a career-best 150 runs. In 2006, he batted a career-best .330 for the Orioles. He was a four-time All-Star with Baltimore.

Tejada also proved to be remarkably durable. He played 162 games each year for six seasons in a row beginning in 2001 before appearing in only 133 games for the Orioles in '07. That long streak of games played became more of a story when reporters for ESPN presented Tejada and the Orioles with evidence in 2008 that the shortstop really was two years older than previously thought.

The Astros thought they had signed a 31-year-old player to a free-agent contract that year—when he really was 33. Some people felt that he should have signed a new contract, but the Astros didn't seem to mind. In fact, his new club was pleased with his performance: In 2008, Tejada hit .286 for Houston while playing nearly every day at shortstop.

Texas Rangers

Please see pages 10–11.

Third Base

This is the base to the left of home plate if you're looking at the field from behind home plate. As its name says, it is the third stop of four on the way to scoring a run.

Third base also can refer to a place in the field. The man who plays third base is the fielder positioned closest to that base. In scorekeeping, the third base position is designated by the number 5.

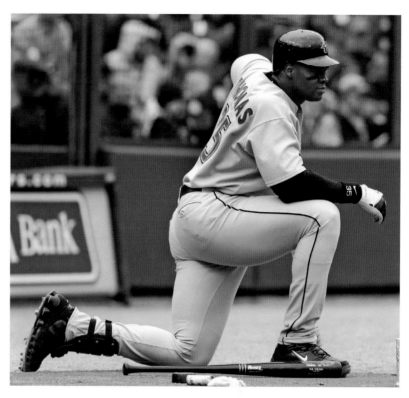

■ *Thomas became one of baseball's best DHs.*

Thomas, Frank

Two-time MVP Frank Thomas was one of the American League's most feared hitters through much of the 1990s and 2000s. At 6 feet 5 inches (2 m) and 257 pounds (117 kg), he was such a huge threat to opposing pitchers that he earned the nickname "The Big Hurt."

In one seven-year stretch for the Chicago White Sox in the 1990s (1991–97), Thomas hit better than .300, scored more than 100 runs, drove in more than 100 runs, and walked more than 100 times each season. He was named the A.L.'s MVP for both 1993 (41 homers, 128 RBI, .317 batting average) and 1994 (38 homers, 101 RBI, .353). In 1997, Thomas won the A.L. batting title with a .347 mark.

A first baseman and designated hitter his entire career, Thomas played 16 seasons for the White Sox before joining the Oakland A's, for whom he hit 39 home runs at age 38 in 2006. In 2007, he hit his 500th career homer while playing for the Toronto Blue Jays. He played for both Toronto and Oakland in an injury-marred 2008 season during which he turned 40 years old.

Thome, Jim

Chicago White Sox designated hitter Jim Thome has been one of the premier sluggers of the 1990s and 2000s. He is a five-time All-Star and a member of the 500 home-run club.

■ *Thome is a top A.L. slugger.*

League's Phillies for 2003. He didn't slow down in Philadelphia, launching 47 homers in 2003 (along with a career-best 131 RBI) and 42 in 2004 before an injury-shortened '05 season. He was back in the American League the next year after a trade to the Chicago White Sox. He was an All-Star designated hitter in his first season in Chicago, when he hit 42 homers and drove in 109 runs in 2006.

The next year, Thome became the 23rd big-leaguer to hit 500 career home runs. He did it in dramatic fashion, launching a game-winning, walk-off home run off the Los Angeles Angels' Dustin Moseley in the bottom of the ninth inning in a game in Chicago.

Tiger Stadium

Tiger Stadium was the home of the American League's Detroit Tigers for 88 seasons—from the time it opened in 1912 through 1999. It originally was called Navin Field, then became Briggs Stadium from 1938 to 1960 before being renamed Tiger Stadium.

The stadium opened the same day in 1912 that Fenway Park opened in Boston. Detroit's stadium featured a second deck in right field that hung over the lower deck by 10 feet. One of the most famous home runs in the park's history came in the 1971 All-Star Game, when the Yankees' Reggie Jackson hit a mammoth blast that struck a transformer above the roof in right field.

Thome began his career as a third baseman for the Cleveland Indians in 1990. After several seasons as a part-time player, he earned a full-time job in 1994 and slammed 20 home runs in the strike-shortened season. After hitting 38 home runs and driving in 116 runs in 1996, he moved to first base the following season and earned his first All-Star nod for a 40-homer, 102-RBI year for the A.L. champs.

In his final season in Cleveland in 2002, the left-handed-hitting Thome belted a club-record 52 home runs. That earned him a big free-agent contract with the National

Another big home run at the site was by New York's Babe Ruth in 1934: his 700th career round-tripper, which cleared the right-field stands—there was no upper deck then—and left the park altogether.

Tiger Stadium hosted the World Series six times (Detroit won four of them) and the All-Star Game three times (1941 and 1951, in addition to '71). The NFL's Detroit Lions also played home games at the park from 1938 to 1974 before moving into the new Pontiac Silverdome. The Tigers moved into their new stadium, Comerica Park, in April of 2000.

Time Out

A time out is a stoppage in play signaled by an umpire. Time outs in baseball are different from those in other major sports because teams are not given a specific allotment to use. Instead, baseball time outs can only be called by an umpire, although a manager, coach, batter, or other player may request them.

Tinker to Evers to Chance

This is the most famous double-play combination ever. Shortstop Joe Tinker, second baseman Johnny Evers, and first baseman Frank Chance played together for the Chicago Cubs in the early 1900s.

The trio first played together in the Cubs' infield on September 2, 1902. In 1910, the three players were immortalized in a poem by Franklin Pierce Adams.

continued on page 18

■ *The corner of Michigan and Trumbull will always be special to Detroit fans as the Tigers' old home.*

Toronto Blue Jays

The Toronto Blue Jays are the only team outside of the United States to win the World Series. The Blue Jays were baseball's champs in 1992 and 1993.

Toronto's Major League history dates to 1977, although the history of baseball in Canada goes back to the 1870s. In 1977, eight years after the National League placed a team in Montreal, the American League placed a team in Toronto, Ontario, Canada.

■ *In 1992, Joe Carter enjoyed the ride.*

The early Blue Jays' teams were not good, which was typical of expansion clubs of the time. They had to rely mostly on young players who were not quite ready for the Major Leagues and older players who were just trying to hang on for another year or two, but who might otherwise be out of baseball. New rules and the free-agent market made it easier for later expansion teams to be competitive faster—almost from the start.

One of Toronto's first real stars was pitcher right-hander Dave Stieb, who made his big-league debut in 1979 and was an All-Star the next season for the first of five times. Stieb spent almost all of his 16-year career with the Blue Jays, and he won 175 games for the club. He was a 17-game winner for Toronto's 1983 team, which surprised baseball by posting a winning record 89–73 for the first time and remaining in the A.L. East title chase for most of the summer under second-year manager Bobby Cox.

Two years later, the Blue Jays weren't just contenders, but were division champions after winning a club-record 99 games. Stieb, who led the American League with an ERA of 2.48, was joined by 17-game winner Doyle Alexander and 14-game winner Jimmy Key on an excellent pitching staff. The offense was led by the power-hitting outfield trio of George Bell, Jesse Barfield, and Lloyd Moseby.

Despite a seven-game loss to Kansas City in the American League Championship Series, that season marked the beginning of good times. Toronto went on to win the A.L. East four more times by 1993.

The fans started coming out to Exhibition Stadium in droves. Then they really turned out when the team moved into the new SkyDome in June of 1989. The SkyDome was the first of baseball's retractable-roof stadiums. That means the roof can stay open in good weather or close in bad weather. The SkyDome was such a big hit that in 1991, the Blue Jays became the first team ever to draw more than 4 million fans in a season.

Toronto was a big on the field, too. In 1992, the Blue Jays won another A.L. East title behind pitcher Jack Morris' 21 wins and outfielder Dave Winfield's 108 RBI.

That made the Blue Jays the first Canadian team to play in the World Series. They were the first to win it, too, downing the N.L.'s Atlanta Braves in six games.

How do you top that? Well, you win it again the next year. The Blue Jays not only repeated as World Series champs in 1993, but they did it in dramatic fashion.

Toronto held a three-games-to-two edge over Philadelphia in the World Series.

The Phillies led Game 6, though, 6–5 in the bottom of the ninth inning when Joe Carter stepped to the plate for the Blue Jays with two out and two men on base. Carter launched a pitch from Philadelphia closer Mitch Williams for a three-run home run to win the Series! Carter danced around the bases after one of the baseball's memorable home runs.

■ *A.J. Burnett is a Blue Jays ace.*

TORONTO BLUE JAYS

LEAGUE: **AMERICAN**

DIVISION: **EAST**

YEAR FOUNDED: **1977**

CURRENT COLORS: **LIGHT BLUE AND RED**

STADIUM (CAPACITY): **ROGERS CENTRE (50,516)**

ALL-TIME RECORD (THROUGH 2008): **2,514–2,545**

WORLD SERIES TITLES (MOST RECENT): **2 (1993)**

Since then, the Blue Jays have had some pretty good players such as Cy Young Award-winning pitchers Pat Hentgen 1996, Roger Clemens 1997 and 1998, and Roy Halladay 2003, plus slugger Carlos Delgado.

But while the Boston Red Sox and the New York Yankees have dominated the A.L. East over the past 15 years or so, Toronto is still looking to bring the playoffs back to Canada.

"Baseball's Sad Lexicon," which first ran in the *New York Evening Mail*, was about the New York Giants' pennant chances being ruined by Chicago's ability to turn the double play. The Cubs won the N.L. pennant that year, finishing 13 games ahead of the second-place Giants.

Fittingly, Tinker, Evers, and Chance all were inducted into the National Baseball Hall of Fame in the same class 1946. However, historians say the voting was greatly helped by Adams' poem.

■ *A catcher shows off the "tools of ignorance."*

"Tools of Ignorance"

The Tools of Ignorance are a catcher's gear—the glove, mask (including helmet), chest protector, and shin guards. It's a joking, slang name for the gear, with the joke being that a player should be smarter than to want to take on the difficult job of playing catcher.

The origin of the term "Tools of Ignorance" is uncertain. Some reports credit it to Bill Dickey, a Hall-of-Fame catcher for the Yankees from 1928 to 1946, and some to Muddy Ruel, another big-league catcher from 1915 to 1934.

Toronto Blue Jays

Please see pages 16–17.

Torre, Joe

Many baseball fans know Joe Torre as one of the most successful managers ever. But before that, he also was a nine-time All-Star catcher and infielder and a National League MVP. In all, he has spent nearly 50 years in big-league baseball.

Torre was only 19 when he made his debut with the Milwaukee Braves in 1960. The next year, he hit .278 and was second in the rookie-of-the-year balloting; by 1963, he was an All-Star for the first time.

In 1964, Torre batted .321 with 20 homers and 109 RBI. It was the first of his six seasons with 20 or more homers—topped by 36 in 1966—and five years with 100 or more

RBI. He put it all together in 1971, when he hit a league-leading .363 for the St. Louis Cardinals with 24 home runs and 137 RBI, another N.L. best. Originally a catcher who was good enough to start four times at the position in the All-Star Game and earn a Gold Glove in 1965, he gradually shifted to third base and first base. He started a pair of All-Star Games at third.

In his final season in 1977, Torre had only 51 at-bats while playing for the New York Mets. But after the club got off to a poor start that year, Torre took over as manager and began a long career in that capacity. He had five uneventful seasons with the Mets, but was hired in Atlanta in 1982 and led the Braves to a division championship in the first of his three years there.

Torre also managed in St. Louis for six seasons before his great success with the Yankees. He took over New York in 1996 and led the club to its first World Series victory in 18 years. The Yankees won it all again two years later to begin a string of three championships in a row.

In 12 seasons with the Yankees, Torre guided his teams to the playoffs each year. Under his watch, New York won 10 division titles and six A.L. pennants.

In 2008, Torre moved back to the National League to become the manager of the Los Angeles Dodgers. He led them to an N.L. West Division title and a spot in the NLCS, too.

■ *Torre's Dodgers won the N.L. West in 2008.*

Total Bases

This is a statistical category for batting that measures the number of bases produced by a player's hits. Every single is worth one base, every double is worth two bases, every triple is worth three bases, and a home run is worth four bases.

A player's slugging percentage is figured by taking the number of total bases and dividing by the number of official at-bats.

■ *Trainers treat any player who is injured.*

instance in 1962, catcher Harry Chiti was traded in April from the Cleveland Indians to the New York Mets for a player to be named later. In June, Chiti turned out to be the player named later—making him the only player in baseball history to be traded for himself!

Trainer

A trainer is a member of a baseball team's support staff. He or she is not a doctor, but does have some medical skills and can treat minor injuries. The trainer also helps players with daily activities such as their workout routine, rehabilitation from injuries, and nutrition.

Triple

A triple is a hit on which the batter makes it all the way to third base without an error by the fielding team. Less commonly, it is called a "three-base hit."

A triple is one of the most exciting plays in baseball because it typically takes a speedy runner to make it all the way to third base. Triples are also less common than any other type of hit.

Triple Crown

The Triple Crown is not a real award or trophy, but is a special statistic reserved for players who lead their league in batting average, home runs, and runs batted in during the same season. It's a rare feat,

Trade

When a player or several players are exchanged between big-league organizations. Players can be traded for other players, for draft picks, or for cash. Teams trade for players that will help their team. Most teams try to create fair trades that help both teams. Sometimes a team will trade for a player for just part of a season in an effort to make a run at the pennant.

Sometimes, a player is traded for a "player to be named later." In one unusual accomplished by only a select few players in baseball history.

There have been only 13 Triple Crown winners since 1900, and none since Boston's Carl Yastrzemski in 1967. (See a complete list on page 81.) The only players to earn the Triple Crown more than once are two-time winners Rogers Hornsby and Ted Williams. Every Triple Crown winner since 1900 is in the Hall of Fame.

"Pitching's Triple Crown" is sometimes won, too. That means a pitcher has led his league in wins, strikeouts, and earned-run average in the same season. It's a bit more common occurrence, and last was achieved by San Diego's Jake Peavy in 2007.

(That play came all the way back in 1920. It was made by Cleveland's Bill Wambsganss.) The latest unassisted triple play was in 2008 by Cleveland's Asdrubal Cabrera. With runners on first and second, Cabrera made a diving catch. He stepped on second base for the second out and tagged the runner who had been on first for the third out. Both runners had been going on the pitch and had gotten too far from their bases. (See a list of all these plays on page 82.)

In 1990, against Boston, the Minnesota Twins became the first team in big-league history to pull off two triple plays in the same game. Both triple plays were started by third baseman Gary Gaetti.

Triple Play

This is a rare happening in which the defense records three outs on a single play. By definition, there must be no outs for a triple play to occur. Many triple plays come with runners on first and second base. A line drive is caught by a middle infielder, and the runners are trapped too far off the base to get back safely.

Unassisted triple plays are the rarest of all. These are triple plays in which one defensive player records all the outs himself. There have been only 13 unassisted triple plays during the regular season in Major League history, plus one in the World Series.

■ *Yaz's Triple Crown numbers: .326, 44 homers, and 126 RBI.*

Uecker, Bob

Bob Uecker is in the Hall of Fame, but he'll be the first to tell you it's not because of his playing ability. Uecker was a pretty poor catcher in his brief pro career, but he found new life in the broadcast booth. As a radio and TV voice for the Milwaukee Brewers since 1971, he has become famous for his humorous ways of describing baseball games. He has also appeared in many national commercials, in movies, and even was an actor in a long-running TV show, *Mr. Belvedere*. For a guy who hit .200 in the Majors, he's had a pretty good career in baseball.

Uncle Charlie

A slang term for a curveball. From the letter "c" for curveball.

Uniform

The official team gear that a player wears during a game. This includes the jersey top, an undershirt, pants, a belt, socks, and a cap. Players can usually choose their own cleats to wear, though many teams make their players' cleats match. The Oakland A's, for instance, almost always wear white cleats.

Uniforms have changed quite a bit over the years in baseball. The first players wore long pants and long-sleeved shirts with vests. The first caps were round with a flat top and a short brim. Knee-length "knick-ers" were first used in the 1860s. Some players today still wear these, and you see their entire team-colored sock on their calf. Most players today, however, prefer longer pants that reach their shoe tops.

An interesting uniform note is that baseball is the only pro sport that rules that its managers and coaches must wear the same uniform as the players. If a manager chooses to wear a business suit, as longtime manager Connie Mack did, he may not go on the field during a game.

Utility Player

Most players specialize at one defensive position, but utility players have a bag full of baseball gloves. Utility players give a team flexibility and the chance to try many lineups. A utility player might start a game in left field, then switch to second base later on. Some utility players can also play catcher.

Utley, Chase

A power-hitting second baseman is a rare thing, but Chase Utley has become one of baseball's best players by being just that. He burst onto the scene in 2005, hitting 28 homers in only 96 games. He's been an All-Star ever since, topping 100 RBI four times while regularly batting above .300. He helped the Phillies win two N.L. East titles and then, in 2008, their first World Series title since 1980.

Umpires

The only other people on a baseball field beside the players are the umpires. These experts have the job of calling balls and strikes, deciding if a player is out or safe, if a ball is caught, etc. In other words, they enforce the rules of the game.

The main umpire usually works behind home plate. He stands or squats behind the catcher and decides if a pitch is a ball or strike. The home-plate umpire wears a metal mask, a chest protector, shin guards, and shoes with heavy steel toes. He has extra baseballs in a bag.

Other umpires (depending on the level of play) are arranged around the field. At the Major League level, there is an umpire at each of the bases. They wear the same uniform as the home-plate umpire. (Trivia time: You can call any umpire by the nickname "Blue" due to the dark-blue shirts often worn by big-league umps.)

Like the ballplayers, the umpires work as a team, moving around the field to follow the action. For instance, if the third-base umpire has to run down the left-field line to see if a ball is fair or foul, the home-plate umpire might run to third base to await a possible play there. On very tough plays or when rules are questioned, the umpires get together to make their decisions. Beginning in 2008, Major League umpires can check video instant replay on some calls.

When making their calls, umpires use hand signals. Arms swept out to the side mean a player is safe. A fist pump or a thumb lifted upward mean a player is out. A finger waved in a circle means a ball has been hit for a home run.

Umpires have a very hard job, and often have to listen to complaints from players and coaches. If those complaints get out of hand, the umpires can eject the player or coach from the game.

See a list of current umpires on page 83.

■ *The umpire signals that the runner (11) is safe.*

Valenzuela, Fernando

Few players have made as splashy a debut or have had such instant success as this left-handed pitcher from Mexico. Not expected to make the Dodgers' roster in 1981, Valenzuela instead started on Opening Day–and threw a shutout. Fernandomania was born. Over the next few months, he thrilled fans with his dazzling

■ *Fernandomania was a big hit in Los Angeles.*

pitching, winning his first eight starts with an ERA of 0.50. He ended the season 13–7 and was the first player to win both the Cy Young and Rookie of the Year awards. To cap it all off, he helped the Dodgers win the World Series. It was one of the most memorable rookie seasons ever.

Fernando also charmed fans with his ready smile and his unusual windup. As he lifted his leg in the windup, he actually rolled his eyes skyward before swooping in and down to deliver the pitch.

Valenzuela used his rookie season as a springboard to a solid Major League career. Valenzuela had a no-hitter in 1989; his best season was 1986, when he was 21–10 with a 3.14 ERA. He went on to play for six teams. A highlight came in 1996, when he pitched for the San Diego Padres in the first official MLB game played in Mexico. (He beat the Mets that day.) Valenzuela retired in 1997 but still pitched in Mexican leagues occasionally after that.

Vander Meer, Johnny

Vander Meer will forever be known for one thing–or should we say two? In 1938, the Cincinnati Reds left hander became the first, and still only, pitcher to throw no-hitters in back-to-back starts. First, he held the Boston Braves from getting a hit on June 11, while walking only three batters. On June 15, during the first night game ever at Brooklyn's Ebbets Field, he repeated the feat. He walked eight in the game, but allowed no hits–again. A good catch on the final batter by center fielder Harry Craft saved this amazing record.

Vander Meer remained an effective pitcher, leading the National League in strikeouts and wins three times. His pitching was also wild, and his career record of 119–121 shows it. However, he'll always have those two games in 1938.

Veeck, Bill Jr.

Few people had more fun–or created more fun–in baseball than Bill Veeck ("as in 'wreck,'" he used to say). Veeck was a team owner and executive for several teams beginning in 1930 and was part of baseball for more than 50 years. Throughout his career, he worked to make the ballpark experience more fun for fans.

Veeck's father, Bill Sr., worked for the Chicago Cubs, and Bill Jr. was 11 when he first started working in baseball. After college, he stayed on with the Cubs. His biggest move with the Cubs was to plant ivy along the brick outfield wall of Wrigley Field . . . ivy that still grows there today. When he was 27, he bought a minor-league team, the Milwaukee Brewers. He started some games at 8:30 A.M. to help overnight workers see a game. He gave away live lobsters and had live music.

Veeck served in the Marines during World War II and lost his right leg in battle.

In 1946, with some partners, he bought the Cleveland Indians. His ideas helped the team set attendance records, and they also won a World Series in 1948. He sold the club two years later, but bought the St. Louis Browns in 1951. He pulled off

■ *Veeck made sure fans had fun at his teams' games.*

his most famous trick there, hiring a small circus performer, Eddie Gaedel, to appear as a batter for the Browns.

Baseball's other owners didn't always like Veeck's ideas. When he tried to move the Browns to Baltimore, they said the team could move–if Veeck sold it. He did, but he bought the Chicago White Sox in 1959. There he installed Comiskey Park's famous exploding scoreboard. Fireworks went off every time the ChiSox scored.

For his love of the fans, his ground-breaking creativity, and his success as an executive, Veeck was named to the Hall of Fame in 1991.

Veteran

Any player who is beyond his first season is considered a veteran. Usually, the term is used for players with several years of service.

■ *Waddell: Great pitcher, odd guy.*

Waddell, Rube

Rube Waddell was a great pitcher, but he was a pretty strange human being. With the Athletics, he led the A.L. in strikeouts every year from 1902 through 1907. His 349 strikeouts in 1903 were a record until Sandy Koufax struck out 382 in 1965. Waddell helped Philadelphia win the 1905 A.L. pennant, and in 1908, he struck out a then-record 16 batters in one game.

However, he drove his managers crazy. He thought nothing of leaving a game to chase a fire truck as it roared past the ballpark. He would vanish between starts, going fishing or hunting but not bothering to tell anyone on his team. He was fined and suspended for drinking too much or staying out too late, but he just kept it up. Still, he could strike out batters and win games: He won at least 19 games in six seasons. Waddell ended his career in 1910, and died two years later of a fever caught while helping save a friend's house from a flood. He was named to the Hall of Fame in 1946.

Walk

When a player gets four balls during an at-bat, he is awarded first base. This "base on balls" is also known as a walk.

Walker, Moses Fleetwood

In the late 1880s, the National League was the only true "Major" league. However, the American Association was also a very prominent pro league, and some historians call it "Major." Why is this important? Because when Walker played for the Toledo team in the American Association, he made history as the last African-American player at baseball's Major-League level. He was a catcher in 1884 with Toledo and later with Newark of the International League. But by 1887, enough white players objected to playing with black players that team owners

Wagner, Honus

At most positions in baseball, recent players have come along to outshine the players from baseball's early years. Barry Bonds has topped Babe Ruth in some ways, Mike Piazza has outhit Mickey Cochrane, Roger Clemens compares to Walter Johnson. However, at shortstop, one player from the early 1900s remains at the top: Honus Wagner. No shortstop since has combined offensive firepower with defense excellence and base-path success as "The Dutchman" did. Wagner was actually a German-American. The word *Deutsch* (DOYTCH) means "German," but fans of the time mispronounced it. Wagner was one of the first five players named to the Hall of Fame, and he remains among the top 20 of many offensive categories nearly 100 years after his career ended in 1917.

Wagner batted above .300 in 16 seasons for a lifetime .327 average. He topped 50 steals five times and finished with 722, trailing only Ty Cobb until their records were broken later. Wagner topped the 100-RBI mark nine times. He led the league in average eight times, a National League record. He also led in slugging average six times.

Wagner started his career with the Louisville Colonels, moving to the Pirates in 1900. With Pittsburgh, he led the N.L. in batting every year but one from 1903 through 1909. In 1909, he led Pittsburgh to a rare World Series title. Wagner hit .333 in the Series with six RBI as the Pirates topped Ty Cobb's Tigers.

Wagner played the game hard, with speed, power, and intensity. A famous story—never really proven—was that his hands were so big and he played so hard that he would often scoop up big handfuls of dirt when fielding grounders, tossing dirt, pebbles, ball, and all to first base.

Wagner retired in 1917 after 21 seasons, and became a much-loved coach in Pittsburgh for 18 years.

■ *Great at everything he did: Honus Wagner.*

decided to ban black players. With that unfair decision, baseball's most shameful period began—the time of the "color barrier." After "Fleet" Walker left baseball, he became the last African-American ballplayer until Jackie Robinson in 1947.

■ *Ward was a leader on and off the field.*

Waner, Lloyd and Paul

Lots of brothers grow up playing baseball together, but Lloyd and Paul Waner grew up to become All-Star hitters and members of the Hall of Fame together. Both were very fast, good hitters, and great on defense in the outfield. Lloyd set a rookie record with 223 hits in 1927, while Paul led the league in triples twice. Lloyd topped .300 10 times and finished with a career mark of .316, but Paul beat that with 13 .300-plus seasons and a career mark of .333. They played together in the Pirates' outfield for most of their career until the duo was broken up in 1941.

They are also well known for their unique nicknames: Big Poison (Paul) and Little Poison (Lloyd). However, they didn't get it for being poisonous to the opposition. When they visited Brooklyn, a fan said—in a thick accent—that every time he looked up, "There's a big poyson [person] on first and a little poyson on second!" From that came the Waners' famous nicknames.

Ward, John

In a long career on and off the field, John Ward did just about everything a person could do in baseball. He started out as a top pitcher; in fact, he threw the second perfect game ever in 1880 while with Providence. But he got a sore arm, so he switched to shortstop and the outfield. He was a speedy runner and good bunter and played enough in the field to top 2,000 career hits. He also led the league in putouts and fielding percentage while playing shortstop with the New York Giants.

But his influence went beyond the playing field. While with the Giants, he got a law degree. He then formed the first players' union, the Brotherhood of Professional Base Ball Players, in 1885. By 1890, Ward was still playing, but was also leading the players in a mini-revolt against the team owners. He helped form the short-lived Players League in 1890. By 1892, the league was dead, but Ward was still a good player and the Giants' manager, too. He led them to a victory in the Temple Cup, a forerunner of the World Series.

Ward retired quite suddenly in 1894 but became a successful lawyer, often involved in baseball matters. This multi-talented person was elected to the Hall of Fame in 1964.

■ *The dirt strip beneath the wall is the warning track.*

Warning Track

The narrow band of dirt that rings a baseball field. The main reason for the track is to let outfielders know when they are approaching the wall. They are looking up at the ball while running to catch it; the feel of dirt beneath their feet lets them know they should slow down to avoid running into the wall. A similar band, made of dirt or some sort of rubberized mat, is found in front of the dugouts to help catchers and infielders. "Warning-track power" means a player hits the ball well, but sometimes not well enough to get the ball out of the ballpark for a home run.

Washington Nationals
Please see pages 30–31.

Washington Senators (Rangers)
Please see Texas Rangers.

Washington Senators (Twins)
Please see Minnesota Twins.

Washington Nationals

The Washington Nationals have only been called that since 2005. Before that, they were the Montreal Expos. So to learn the history of this franchise, one has to go north. In 1969, the Expos became the first-ever Major League team outside the United States. The team was named for an event called Expo67, held two years earlier in Montreal. The Expos were the first team to have their games broadcast in French and English, the two languages spoken in that part of Canada.

The new team didn't have much success in any language for its first several years. They played in Jarry Park, which was supposed to be a temporary home, until 1977.

■ *The Nationals' former home was Montreal.*

They had a few stars in those early years. Mike Marshall set a Major League record by pitching in 92 games in 1973, and Steve Rogers was also a top pitcher. In 1977, though, the team moved into enormous Olympic Stadium, built for the 1976 Summer Games. By 1979, the Expos were contending for the N.L. East title, thanks to young players such as Ellis Valentine, Gary Carter, and Lance Parrish. In 1981, the season was cut in two by a players' strike. The Expos were good enough to make the playoffs, however, but lost in the N.L. Championship Series to the Dodgers.

The 1980s were not that successful, however. Tim Raines was a speedy outfielder and Tim Wallach a good-hitting third baseman. But they were never in the pennant race.

In 1994, a strike again affected another good season for the Expos. Pitchers Ken Hill and Dennis Martinez were aces. Cana-

WASHINGTON NATIONALS	
LEAGUE:	**NATIONAL**
DIVISION:	**EAST**
YEAR FOUNDED:	**1969**
CURRENT COLORS:	**RED, WHITE, AND BLUE**
STADIUM (CAPACITY):	**NATIONALS PARK (41,222)**
ALL-TIME RECORD (THROUGH 2008):	**3,039–3,306**
WORLD SERIES TITLES:	**NONE**

dian-born outfielder Larry Walker both hit for power and played outstanding outfield defense. Montreal was seeing its best team yet. On August 12, the Expos had the best record in the Majors—but the season ended due to the strike. There were no playoffs and no World Series.

In 1997, Pedro Martinez brought Canada its first big award, as he went 17–8 with a 1.90 ERA to win the Cy Young Award, but he signed with Boston in the offseason. Vladimir Guerrero was a big slugger in the late 1990s, earning four All-Star berths; he, too, left after 2003.

In 2002, the Expos were sold. The owner was not an individual, but Major League Baseball itself. No one had come forward when Jeffrey Loria wanted to sell the team and buy the Marlins, so baseball itself stepped in.

In 2005, the Expos left Canada and set up shop in Washington D.C. as the Nationals. They had a great first half of their first season there, but fell to .500. In 2006, they weren't much better, but talented second baseman Alfonso Soriano joined the 40-40 club with 46 homers and 41 steals. (He then left for the Cubs.)

The Nationals remain a middle-of-the-pack team with a few bright lights as they continue to work to bring a championship to the nation's capital.

■ *Cristian Guzman is a bright spot for the Nationals.*

Whiff

A slang term for a strikeout. The word comes from the whistling sound the bat sometimes makes when a batter swings and misses a pitch.

"Who's on First?"

A skit performed first in the 1940s by the comedy team of Bud Abbott and Lou Costello. Costello asks Abbott about the strange nicknames of some players. The first baseman's name is "Who," and this leads to a long, confusing list of other players' names, such as "What," "I Don't Know," and even "Tomorrow." Video clips of this famous bit can often be seen on stadium scoreboards before games, and it plays regularly at the Baseball Hall of Fame. Check out the full "lineup" from the skit on page 84.

Wild Card

Beginning in 1995, baseball reorganized its teams. It switched from two divisions in each league to three. The three division champs made the playoffs, and an additional playoff team from each league was added to make an even four. This added team is the "wild card," the second-place team with the best overall record. Several wild-card teams have gone on to win the World Series, including the Boston Red Sox in 2004 and the Chicago White Sox in 2005.

Williams, Ted

Many experts point to Ted Williams as the best pure hitter in baseball history. Certainly Ted would have said so!

Few players studied the art of hitting as intensely as Williams, and few were better than him at hitting for both average and power. He smacked 521 lifetime home runs, and would surely have had many more had he not spent parts of five seasons as a Navy and Marines fighter pilot in World War II and the Korean War. His lifetime average of .344 includes his amazing 1941 season of .406, when he was the last player to finish above the magic .400 mark. He won six A.L. batting titles and nine slugging-average titles. He played on 19 All-Star teams. Blessed with remarkable vision, he also walked at least 140 times in seven seasons.

Williams, known as "The Splendid Splinter," "Teddy Ballgame," and "The Kid," among other things, won two A.L. MVP awards (1946 and 1949) and probably would have won more had he treated the baseball writers (who vote on the award) a little more kindly. Williams was famously gruff and short-tempered and was quick to challenge anyone who wrote anything negative about him. In fact, he finished second in the voting four times, including once when a writer didn't even give him a 10th-place vote.

Williams grew up in San Diego. He jumped into baseball in 1939 with the Red Sox, setting a rookie record with 145 RBI while batting .327. That was the lowest average he would post until 1949.

Though one of baseball's superstars, he joined the Marines and missed the 1943, 1944, and 1945 seasons due to World War II. He rejoined the military for the Korean War and missed most of 1952 and 1953. In 1957 and 1958, he became the oldest batting champ each year. In 1960, he hit a home run in his final at-bat, leaving the field without tipping his cap to continue a career-long practice.

In 1966, when he was inducted into the Hall of Fame, Williams made a plea for more recognition of Negro League players. Five years later, a special commission did just that and began inducting the greats of those leagues. Williams became a manager briefly, leading the Washington Senators in the early 1970s. He was also a champion fisherman, traveling the world to find new spots to fish. Beloved by baseball, he was honored at the 1999 All-Star Game in Fenway Park, as the stars of that time crowded around to meet their hero.

■ *The sweet swing of the Splendid Splinter.*

■ *Williams was a solid slugger for the Cubs.*

Wild Pitch

When the pitcher delivers a pitch that eludes the catcher in a way that was not the catcher's fault, the official scorer calls the play a "wild pitch." A wild pitch can only happen with runners on base, allowing them to advance. The pitcher does not receive an error on the play. If he throws a pitch past the catcher with no one on base, it's just embarrassing, but doesn't hurt his team.

Williams, Billy

Most fans remember the great Ernie Banks of the Chicago Cubs, but he was joined for many years by another Hall of Famer, outfielder Billy Williams. Williams was a six-time All-Star, hit 426 homers, and won the 1972 batting title. After being tutored in the minors by the great Rogers Hornsby (a Hall-of-Fame player with the Cardinals), Williams was the N.L. Rookie of the Year in 1959 for the Cubs. From 1963 through 1970, Williams didn't miss a game, setting an N.L. consecutive-games streak that lasted until 1983. He was elected to the Hall of Fame in 1987.

Williams, Ted

Please see page 32.

Willis, Dontrelle

Left-hander Dontrelle Willis made a huge splash in the Majors, winning the 2003 N.L. Rookie of the Year award with the Florida Marlins and then helping them win a surprise World Series. In 2005, Willis finished second in the Cy Young voting, going 22–10 with a 2.63 ERA. He was traded to Detroit in 2008.

Willis is also well known for his bubbly personality and his wild delivery. He raises his right knee very high and seems to throw his whole body at the mound with each pitch. He has appeared in several commercials for Major League Baseball.

Wilson, Hack

Hack Wilson's story is one of great success and some tragedy. A powerful slugger for three teams, primarily the Chicago Cubs, he still holds the single-season record with 190 RBI, set in 1930. He was a mighty slugger, whacking 56 homers that year—the second-best mark to Babe Ruth's 60 at the time—and leading the National League in that category four times. However, his drinking off the field and his lack of education made his life after baseball a hard one. Wilson, who was elected to the Hall of Fame in 1979, is remembered today for his short but hugely powerful build and massive arms, as well as his RBI record and sad post-baseball life.

Windup

The motions of the pitcher as he moves his arms, legs, and body to deliver a pitch. Some windups are very elaborate, while others are simple and quick. A pitcher does not use a big windup when runners are on base, which would allow them a better jump in trying to steal a base. But with no runners on, a pitcher winds up and pitches.

Winfield, Dave

How good an athlete was Dave Winfield in his prime? When he left the University of Minnesota in 1973, after winning MVP honors at the College World Series, he was drafted by the Padres, naturally. However, he was also chosen by the Atlanta Hawks of the NBA and the Minnesota Vikings of the NFL. Winfield chose baseball and became one of only a handful of players never to play in the minors. He went right from the Gophers of Minnesota to the Padres of San Diego.

Winfield was good with San Diego, but became a star with the Yankees. Beginning in 1981, he topped 100 RBI with them six

■ *Dontrelle Willis demonstrates his windup.*

times while also winning five Gold Gloves and being named to eight All-Star teams (he was a three-time All-Star with the Padres). However, Winfield fought often with Yankees owner George Steinbrenner about contracts and about Winfield's play. After injuring his back, Winfield left the Yankees in 1991.

Winfield had more highlights after he left the Yankees and Steinbrenner. In 1991, at 39, he became the oldest player to hit for the cycle. In 1992, with the Blue Jays, he doubled home two runs in the 11th inning of Game Six of the World Series, giving Toronto its first championship. And in 1993, back with the hometown Twins, he reached 3,000 hits for his career. Winfield was named to the Hall of Fame in 2001.

Women, Baseball and

No woman has ever played Major League Baseball. However, some women have had an impact on the teams and the game itself.

In baseball's early days, a traveling team of women players was known as the "Bloomers," for the type of long, baggy pants they wore. In the 1940s, while many male players were away on military service, a women's pro league was founded. Teams played first softball and then baseball. The All-American Girls Professional Baseball League lasted from 1943 to 1954. For a complete list of the teams in this league, see page 85. Another women's pro league was around briefly in the 1980s, but it faded quickly.

Girls can play in Little League games. Several have taken part in the annual Little League World Series. Also, young women have taken part in high school and college games.

For many years, there were almost no women involved in baseball business. An exception was Effa Manley,

■ *A play from the All-American Girls Pro Baseball League.*

who, with her husband, ran a Negro League baseball team. For her contributions to those teams, she was made the only woman in the Hall of Fame in 2006.

Marge Schott owned the Cincinnati Reds from 1985 to 1999. Though the Reds won the 1990 World Series, Schott was more known for her odd behavior, including making players pet her dog Schottzie before games.

■ *Cuba (in red) lost to Japan in the final of the 2006 World Baseball Classic.*

Today, some women hold key positions on teams. Kim Ng is an assistant general manager of the Los Angeles Dodgers, which are co-owned by Frank McCourt and his wife, Jamie. The New York Yankees have a female vice-president, Jean Afterman. However, women are far from a big part of today's baseball teams.

Wood, Kerry

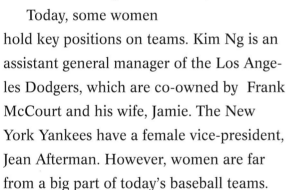 Kerry Wood burst onto the baseball scene in 1998 as a fireballing rookie. On May 6 of that year, he became only the second pitcher ever (after Roger Clemens) to strike out 20 batters in a nine-inning game. Wood was only 20 years old at the time; he was later named the N.L. Rookie of the Year. But he struggled in the coming seasons to match that early success, and arm problems soon derailed his promising

career. Wood battled back and by 2008 had found a new role as the closer for the Cubs, helping that team win the N.L. Central.

World Baseball Classic

A tournament first held in 2006 that matched teams representing individual nations. Japan won that event, defeating Cuba in the final in San Diego. While there have long been international competitions, the WBC was the first that allowed active Major Leaguers to take part for their home countries. Stars such as Ichiro Suzuki (Japan), Ivan Rodriguez (Puerto Rico), Albert Pujols and David Ortiz (Dominican Republic), and Derek Jeter and Alex Rodriguez (United States) took part in the two-week event. The next WBC was scheduled to be played in the spring of 2009.

World Series 1903-1909: Let's Get Started!

When the American League started in 1901 to challenge the older National League, pretty soon people wanted the two leagues' champions to meet. There had been events called "World Series" in the 1880s and 1890s, but they didn't match the champions of two Major Leagues. They were smaller affairs, sometimes featuring two teams from the same league.

In 1903, what we know today as the World Series was born. After much discussion between the two league presidents, the two leagues' top teams agreed to meet to determine one overall champ. Some supporters of the older N.L. (founded in 1876) didn't think their teams should "stoop" to playing the younger A.L. teams. But team owners knew that such a series would generate cash and fan interest. Boston won the first World Series, defeating the Pittsburgh Pirates.

The following year, John T. Brush and John McGraw, the owner and manager,

■ *Before a 1903 World Series game in Boston, fans swarmed onto the field.*

respectively of the N.L.-champion New York Giants, refused to play Boston, again the A.L. champion. Only a year old, and the World Series was already a controversy! In 1905, the Giants gave in and played. Baseball fans watched history being made. The Giants' Christy Mathewson pitched three shutouts in six days. He allowed 14 hits and only one walk in 27 innings, while striking out 18. The Giants won in five games.

The 1906 Series was an all-Chicago event. The Cubs of the N.L. had set a record with 116 wins that year, while the White Sox of the A.L. had won despite batting only .228. These "Hitless Wonders," as they were known, surprised everyone by knocking off the mighty Cubs in six games. The Cubs got their championship the following season, defeating the Detroit Tigers in five games.

The Cubs made it two in a row the following season. This time, they were led by "Three-Finger" Brown's two victories and the

■ *Wagner won his only Series title in 1909.*

great hitting of first baseman Frank Chance. However, this was the last World Series triumph for the Cubs in the 20th century.

The Tigers, after losing the previous two World Series, hoped to end the string in 1909. This Series matched up two of baseball's all-time superstars: Ty Cobb of Detroit and Honus Wagner of Pittsburgh. Cobb longed for a championship to go with his many records. Wagner, the steady old pro, knew this was probably his last chance.

In a seven-game thriller—the first Series to go the full seven games—both teams played well. But amid all the star power, Pittsburgh rookie Babe Adams was the hero, with three wins.

YEAR	WINNING TEAM	LOSING TEAM	RESULT (GAMES)
1903	Boston Red Sox	Pittsburgh Pirates	5–3
1904	World Series not played		
1905	New York Giants	Philadelphia Athletics	4–1
1906	Chicago White Sox	Chicago Cubs	4–2
1907	Chicago Cubs	Detroit Tigers	4–0
1908	Chicago Cubs	Detroit Tigers	4–1
1909	Pittsburgh Pirates	Detroit Tigers	4–3

World Series 1910-1919: The Black Sox

Two teams, led by legendary baseball names, dominated the World Series in this decade. But it was off-the-field events that dominated the headlines.

Manager/owner Connie Mack led the Athletics to World Series titles in 1910, 1911, and 1913. Among the stars for those teams were Hall of Famers Eddie Collins, Chief Bender, and Frank "Home Run" Baker. Mack was well-known as a great judge of talent, but had never taken a team to the title before 1910. He was also famous for his habit of wearing a business suit to manage games. All other managers, then and now, wore the same uniforms as their teams. Due to baseball rules, Mack couldn't even go on the field during a game while in his suit.

He didn't need to, with such great players. The Athletics defeated the Cubs twice and the Giants once to win three World Series in four seasons.

Meanwhile, the city of Boston enjoyed five World Series championships in the decade. They got four of them from the Red Sox (1912, 1915, 1916, and 1918). The latter three of those were paced by a young left-handed pitcher named Babe Ruth, who was a pretty fair hitter as well. In 1916 and 1918, Ruth put together a string of 29.1 innings without allowing a run, a World Series record that stood until the Yankees' Whitey Ford broke it in 1961. With Ruth setting pitching records as well as slugging home runs, the Red Sox were the cream of the A.L.

Of special note was the other Boston championship team, the 1914 Boston Braves of the N.L. Known as the "Miracle Braves," they were in last place in mid-July, yet roared back to win the pennant by a remarkable 10½ games. In the World Series, they continued their late dominant run by sweeping the mighty Athletics. Catch-

■ *Managers John McGraw (left) and Connie Mack.*

er Hank Gowdy set a record by batting .545 in the Series.

However, events away from the field were gathering to have a big effect on baseball. First, World War I was raging in Europe. In 1917, the United States finally entered on the side of the Allies. Many players, including stars such as Christy Mathewson, went off to war. The games continued, and the White Sox won the Series that year. Like their crosstown rivals, the Cubs, this would be the last championship they would win for a long time (the White Sox next won in 2005). They defeated the New York Giants.

In 1918, the season was cut short by the U.S. government, and the Series was played in early September. The Red Sox won their last title of the 20th century, defeating the Chicago Cubs.

By 1919, however, the war was over, and baseball was back. The mighty White Sox, led by stars such as outfielder "Shoeless Joe" Jackson and ace pitcher Eddie Cicotte, were expected to beat the N.L.-champion Cincinnati Reds easily. However, Chicago lost in eight games (the Series was best-of-nine for several years). Based on the actions of some players and other evidence, some experts suspected something fishy.

After an investigation, in late 1920, eight players from the White Sox were banned from baseball for "throwing" the Series. That is, they lost on purpose, paid by gamblers. "Shoeless Joe" was among the eight, though some feel he was unfairly included, as it was never proven that he took money and that he played his best (he batted .375 in the Series), but he remains out of the Hall of Fame.

By this time in its history, the World Series had reached an enormous national popularity. The "Black Sox" scandal of 1919 tarnished the World Series and baseball badly. To recover, the game needed a new hero to thrill the fans. In the 1920s, they got that hero—and it turned out to be a pitcher they knew very well.

YEAR	WINNING TEAM	LOSING TEAM	RESULT (GAMES)
1910	Philadelphia Athletics	Chicago Cubs	4-1
1911	Philadelphia Athletics	Chicago Cubs	4-1
1912	Boston Red Sox	New York Giants	4-3-1
1913	Philadelphia Athletics	New York Giants	4-1
1914	Boston Braves	Philadelphia Athletics	4-0
1915	Boston Red Sox	Philadelphia Athletics	4-1
1916	Boston Red Sox	Brooklyn Dodgers	4-1
1917	Chicago White Sox	New York Giants	4-2
1918	Boston Red Sox	Chicago Cubs	4-2
1919	Cincinnati Reds	Chicago White Sox	5-3

World Series 1920-1929: The Yankee Years

Following the "Black Sox" scandal of the 1919 World Series (eight White Sox players were kicked out of baseball for accepting bribes to lose on purpose), baseball had to battle to regain the public's trust. The scandal of the 1919 Series didn't fully come out until late in the 1920 season. Thus fans could enjoy, worry-free, the amazing events of the 1920 Series. In Game Five, Cleveland's Bill Wambsganss pulled off a memorable feat. After snagging a line drive by Brooklyn's Clarence Mitchell, "Wamby" stepped on second to double off one runner, then tagged a runner who had broken from first on the hit. It was an unassisted triple play, still the only one in World Series history. The Indians went on to win in seven games.

The following year, 1921, the baseball world was awash in talk of the Black Sox—and along came a big distraction. Babe Ruth had earned World Series glory as a pitcher with the Red Sox in the 1910s. Sold to the Yankees before the 1920 season, he had turned the baseball world on its ear with his mammoth—and numerous—home runs. By 1921, he had carried the Yankees to their first World Series appearance on the strength of his league-record 54 homers. However, though Ruth got his first Series homer, the New York Giants beat the Yanks in eight games (all of which were played at one ballpark, the Polo Grounds—a Series first). The same teams met in 1922 with the Giants winning again.

In 1923, however, the legend of Ruth added a new page. The Yankees opened their new Yankee Stadium, and Ruth brought the World Series to his fans for the third straight year. This time, they beat the Giants, as Ruth hit three homers and pitcher Herb Pennock won two games for the Yanks.

The 1924 Series featured another legend, Washington pitcher Walter Johnson. Near the end of his great

■ *Action from the 1921 Yankees-Giants Series.*

career, this was the only Series title for "The Big Train." He played a big part, coming into the seventh game on only one day of rest to win the finale in relief. In 1925, Johnson got a chance for two titles in a row, but his Senators fell to the Pirates.

Ruth was the goat, not the hero, in 1926, when he was called out trying to steal second for the last out of Game Seven. It was a tough way to end the Series, especially as he had clubbed four homers.

■ *The World Series was first heard on radio in 1922.*

In 1927, he more than made up for it. Joined again by young slugger Lou Gehrig, Ruth led one of the finest teams of all time into a sweep over the Pirates. (Said one writer about the matchup, "If the Pirates ain't scared, they ain't human.")

After bashing an astounding 60 homers in the 1927 regular season, Ruth added two more in the Series. In 1928, the Yanks made it two sweeps in a row (this time over the Cardinals). Gehrig matched Ruth's record of four homers and added nine RBI.

The decade ended with a return to glory for Connie Mack and the Athletics. Though the A's had stars such as Jimmie Foxx and Al Simmons, it was pitcher Howard Ehmke who got them off to a good start. The turning point came when the A's scored 10 runs in the seventh inning of Game Five to rally from an 8–0 deficit.

YEAR	WINNING TEAM	LOSING TEAM	RESULT (GAMES)
1920	Cleveland Indians	Brooklyn Dodgers	5-2
1921	New York Giants	New York Yankees	5-3
1922	New York Giants	New York Yankees	4-0-1
1923	New York Yankees	New York Giants	4-2
1924	Washington Senators	New York Giants	4-3
1925	Pittsburgh Pirates	Washington Senators	4-3
1926	St. Louis Cardinals	New York Yankees	4-3
1927	New York Yankees	Pittsburgh Pirates	4-0
1928	New York Yankees	St. Louis Cardinals	4-0
1929	Philadelphia Athletics	Chicago Cubs	4-1

World Series 1930-1939: A Mighty Dynasty

The Athletics started the 1930s as they ended the 1920s, by winning the World Series. They were led by the sterling pitching of Lefty Grove and George Earnshaw, who each won two games as Philadelphia beat the Cardinals, and the hitting of Al Simmons and Jimmie Foxx.

■ *Gehrig (left) greeted Ruth after a 1932 homer—then hit one, too.*

The Cardinals got their revenge the following year, winning a seven-game thriller. The hero was outfielder Pepper Martin, who batted .500 with a homer and five clutch RBI.

The 1932 Series featured one of baseball's most memorable moments. The trouble is, no one can agree on what actually happened. Here's the situation: Fifth inning of Game Three at Wrigley Field as the hometown Cubs face the mighty New York Yankees. New York was already ahead two games to none, and the score in this game was tied 4–4. Up stepped Babe Ruth, who already had a three-run homer in the game. The Cubs were yelling at Ruth, as were the fans. After taking two strikes, and holding up one finger each time, Ruth then, well—no one's quite sure what he did. Some say that he pointed toward center field. Others say he pointed toward the Cubs' dugout to quiet the hecklers. Was he holding up one finger to show that there was one strike left? Whatever he did then, there's no doubt what he did next—hit the next pitch into the bleachers for a homer. The question remains: Did Ruth "call" his shot? Did he tell the Cubs he would hit a homer to center field—and then do just that? Ruth said about the event, "It's a great story, isn't it?" The Yankees won the Series in four games.

The other New York team, the Giants, returned to the top in 1933, defeating the Senators. In 1934, the Cardinals won another title, this time over Detroit. Their Game Seven win was interrupted when angry Detroit fans threw garbage on the field at Joe Medwick; they were mad about a slide Medwick had made against the Tigers earlier —and that their team was down 11-0!

The Detroit Tigers had played in four World Series, and lost them all, before finally winning a title in 1935. They knocked off the Cubs in six games, led by a pair of great-hitting Hall of Famers, second baseman Charlie Gehringer and catcher Mickey Cochrane.

The following year, all other teams faded into second place for the rest of the decade. From 1936–1939, only the New York Yankees were World Series champions. It was the longest streak of success to date in the Fall Classic. With Ruth having retired in 1935, Lou Gehrig was the team leader. He was joined by stars such as second baseman Tony

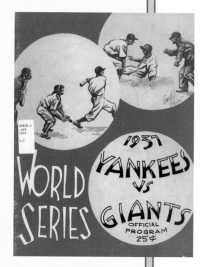

■ *A program from the 1937 Series.*

Lazzeri, catcher Bill Dickey, and pitcher Red Ruffing. But the new superstar in New York was not the soft-spoken Gehrig; it was sweet-swinging center-fielder Joe DiMaggio. "Joltin' Joe" joined the club in 1936 and provided the final piece of the puzzle that would lead to the Yanks' four straight Series wins.

YEAR	WINNING TEAM	LOSING TEAM	RESULT (GAMES)
1930	Philadelphia Athletics	St. Louis Cardinals	4-2
1931	St. Louis Cardinals	Philadelphia Athletics	4-3
1932	New York Yankees	Chicago Cubs	4-0
1933	New York Giants	Washington Senators	4-1
1934	St. Louis Cardinals	Detroit Tigers	4-3
1935	Detroit Tigers	Chicago Cubs	4-2
1936	New York Yankees	New York Giants	4-2
1937	New York Yankees	New York Giants	4-1
1938	New York Yankees	Chicago Cubs	4-0
1939	New York Yankees	Cincinnati Reds	4-0

■ *Back from World War II, Bob Feller drew a crowd to watch him warm up before the 1948 Series.*

World Series 1940-1949: World War II

Shadows fell over the World Series in the 1940s. Beloved star Lou Gehrig of the four-time champion Yankees fell ill and died in 1941. Away from the field fell the heavy shadow of World War II, which the United States entered in late 1941. The Cincinnati Reds had won the 1940 Series over the Tigers, while the Yankees with DiMaggio won yet again in 1941.

However, the next four Series were deeply affected by the war. Hundreds of ballplayers joined the armed forces, many missing prime years of their careers to serve their country. Many saw combat, some were killed or wounded, while others played for military baseball teams to entertain soldiers.

Baseball played on, however, as the U.S. government and President Franklin Roosevelt saw the benefit of home-front workers enjoying a break by watching the games. The Cardinals won the first Series during the war in 1942, defeating the Yankees. Making his Series debut for St. Louis was a left-handed hitter named Stan Musial, soon to become among baseball's best overall players.

Those two teams met again in 1943, though this time Joe DiMaggio, among others, was in a different uniform—that of the

U.S. Army. The Yankees won the rematch behind pitcher Spud Chandler, who was that season's American League MVP. In the Series, he posted a 2-0 mark with a 0.50 ERA.

In 1944, both St. Louis teams made the Series, the Browns from the A.L. for their first and only time. Their crosstown rivals, the Cardinals, led by Musial's .304 average and the pitching of Mort Cooper and Harry Brecheen, won in six games.

In 1945, a war hero became a Series hero. Detroit slugger Hank Greenberg had been one of the first players to sign up for the military. With the war ending in the summer of 1945, he and many other players returned to their teams.

Good thing for Detroit, as Greenberg belted a late-season grand slam to give the Tigers the pennant. Then he hit a pair of homers (and had seven RBI) in their seven-game Series win over the Cubs.

The 1946 Series had one of the most thrilling endings ever. With the Series tied at three games, the Cardinals and Red Sox battled in a fierce Game Seven. Dom DiMaggio, Joe's brother, tied the game with a two-run double in the top of the eighth. In the bottom of the eighth, Del Rice hit a drive to left-center field. Running with the pitch, Enos Slaughter scored the winning run all the way from first. Boston shortstop Johnny Pesky hesitated a moment before throwing the relay in, a mistake for which he would be blamed for years.

The Yankees won it all again in 1947. DiMaggio was back from the war, and he led the team against the Brooklyn Dodgers.

In 1948, Cleveland earned its final Series title of the 20th century, beating the Boston Braves in six games.

The 1940s ended as the 1930s had, with the Yankees winning it all. That 1939 win, however, had ended a streak. Their 1949 World Series title, again over the Dodgers, started a new and amazing run for one of sports' greatest dynasties.

YEAR	WINNING TEAM	LOSING TEAM	RESULT (GAMES)
1940	Cincinnati Reds	Detroit Tigers	4-3
1941	New York Yankees	Brooklyn Dodgers	4-1
1942	St. Louis Cardinals	New York Yankees	4-1
1943	New York Yankees	St. Louis Cardinals	4-1
1944	St. Louis Cardinals	St. Louis Browns	4-2
1945	Detroit Tigers	St. Louis Cardinals	4-3
1946	St. Louis Cardinals	Boston Red Sox	4-3
1947	New York Yankees	Brooklyn Dodgers	4-2
1948	Cleveland Indians	Boston Red Sox	4-2
1949	New York Yankees	Brooklyn Dodgers	4-1

World Series 1950–1959: New York, NY

How's this for a decade of domi-nance? There were 20 spots for teams in the 10 World Series played in the 1950s. Fourteen of those spots went to teams from New York City. Another went to a team that had recently moved out of there. New York teams won eight of those Series. Thanks to the Yankees' powerhouse teams and the hardy Brooklyn Dodgers, New York fans en-joyed a record run of Series to enjoy.

The Yankees carried on where they left off the 1940s, winning in 1950 against the Athletics. The championship was the second of five straight the Yanks would win. Other than the Yankees, who have won three, four, and five straight titles at different times, only the 1972–74 Oakland A's have managed as many as three straight.

Joe DiMaggio helped the Yankees win another title in 1951, but it was his last, as the great "Yankee Clipper" retired after the season. Yogi Berra was one of the stars who remained to carry on the tradition. Berra started out as a catcher and later played outfield, but he was a powerful hitter no matter where he played. He won three A.L. MVPs in the de-cade. Berra ended up play-ing in 10 World Series with the Yankees and still holds a spot at or near the top of many career World Series hitting records.

Stepping in for DiMaggio as the superstar of the Yan-kees was a young Oklaho-man named Mickey Mantle.

■ *Yogi Berra tags a Phillies' runner out during the 1951 Series.*

"The Mick" played with DiMaggio on the '51 champs and made the team his own the next year, helped by his awesomely powerful bat. On the mound, Vic Raschi, Allie Reynolds, and Ed Lopat enjoyed the pleasure of seeing the Yankees' offense give them nice leads to work with. Scrappy infielders Billy Martin and Phil Rizzuto were solid on defense.

■ *Berra couldn't stop this Dodgers' runner in 1955, however.*

They combined to beat the Dodgers again in 1952, with Martin making a game-saving catch of an infield pop by Jackie Robinson in Game Seven.

In 1953, the Dodgers thought they might have the team to end the Yankees' streak. But even Hall of Famers such as Robinson, catcher Roy Campanella, and shortstop Pee Wee Reese were not enough. The Yankees made it five straight World Series titles with a six-game victory.

The 1954 Series featured the third team from New York, the Giants of the N.L. Speedy center fielder Willie Mays electrified the Game One crowd with his amazing over-the-shoulder catch of a long drive by Cleveland's Vic Wertz. Though Wertz's Indians had set a league record with 111 wins, they didn't get even one victory against the Giants, who kept baseball's championship in New York City for the sixth straight season.

After coming close many times, including two recent Series losses to the Yanks, the Brooklyn Dodgers' fans were used to the cry of "Wait 'til next year," heard every year as they lost a final game. In 1955, "next year" finally arrived. Paced by the hitting of Campanella, center fielder Duke Snider, and Robinson, and helped by two wins from right-hander Johnny Podres (including a Game Seven shutout), Brooklyn finally carried the trophy across the East River. (That's the waterway that divides Brooklyn from the Bronx, where the Yankees played, and Manhattan, then home of the Giants.)

In 1956, order was restored, and the Yankees continued their march into history. In Game Five, however, one Yankee gave

World Series 1950-1959: New York, NY, *continued*

■ *Berra leaps, Larsen catches—perfect!*

himself a page all his own in the history books. Right-hander Don Larsen allowed no Dodgers runners to reach base, tossing the only perfect game in World Series history. Larsen was not considered the Yankees' best pitcher—that was Whitey Ford. And only three days earlier, the Dodgers had hit Larsen hard, chasing him from the Game Two in the second inning. So his feat was all the more unexpected. Larsen's perfect game remains among baseball's greatest performances and most memorable games.

Lew Burdette of the Milwaukee Braves put on quite a pitching show himself in the 1957 World Series. He wasn't perfect, but he was pretty close. The righthander won three complete games, allowing only two earned runs and striking out 21 Yankees. The Braves brought Wisconsin its first title.

The Braves couldn't match that feat in 1958, as the Yankees won yet again. This time, pitcher Bob Turley won two games. Hank Bauer smacked four of the Yankees' 10 homers in the seven-game Series. Gil Mc-Dougald, Moose Skowron, and Mantle added a pair of dingers each.

To end the decade, the World Series made its longest trip yet, all the way to the West Coast. The Dodgers had moved to Los Angeles before the 1958 season, and their 1959 N.L. pennant brought the World Series to California for the first time. Their A.L. opponent, the Chicago White Sox, hadn't made the Series since the 1919 "Black Sox" had lost so sadly. The Dodgers showed that the California sun agreed with them, winning in six games. Snider was still around, and was joined by Maury Wills and Jim Gilliam. Pitcher Larry Sherry had two wins and two saves. A highlight was a Game Five attendance of 92,706 at the Los Angeles Memorial Coliseum. That remains the largest crowd ever to see a World Series game.

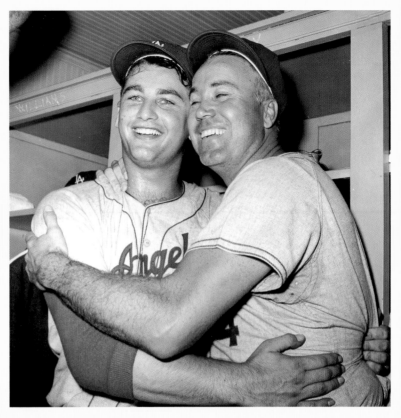

■ *1959 Series MVP Larry Sherry (left) with Duke Snider.*

YEAR	WINNING TEAM	LOSING TEAM	RESULT (GAMES)	MOST VALUABLE PLAYER *
1950	New York Yankees	Philadelphia Athletics	4-0	
1951	New York Yankees	New York Giants	4-2	
1952	New York Yankees	Brooklyn Dodgers	4-3	
1953	New York Yankees	Brooklyn Dodgers	4-2	
1954	New York Giants	Cleveland Indians	4-0	
1955	Brooklyn Dodgers	New York Yankees	4-3	Johnny Podres, Brooklyn P
1956	New York Yankees	Brooklyn Dodgers	4-3	Don Larsen, New York P
1957	Milwaukee Braves	New York Yankees	4-3	Lew Burdette, Milwaukee P
1958	New York Yankees	Milwaukee Braves	4-3	Bob Turley, New York P
1959	Los Angeles Dodgers	Chicago White Sox	4-2	Larry Sherry, Los Angeles P

* Most Valuable Players not named until 1955.

World Series 1960-1969: Arms Race

The 1960s began with a bang, when Pittsburgh's Bill Mazeroski delivered the first World Series-ending, walk-off home run in baseball history. His blast lifted the Pirates over the New York Yankees in a wildly exciting Fall Classic. The rest of the decade, though, belonged to the pitchers. Several outstanding performances highlighted the dominance that pitching held over the game. By late in the 1960s, in fact, pitching had become so overwhelming that Major League Baseball instituted several rules changes (tinkering with the strike zone and lowering the mound) to help hitters.

■ *Pirates' fans celebrated right along with Mazeroski in 1960.*

Mazeroski needed no such help when he came to bat against the Yankees' Ralph Terry in the bottom of the ninth inning of Game Seven of the 1960 World Series with the scored tied 9-9. Although he would bat just .260 during a 17-year career that was notable for his work in the field instead of at the plate, "Maz" had a good Series to that point, with 7 hits in 23 at-bats and four RBI. The really big hitters, however, were all on New York's side. The Yankees had pummeled the Pirates 16-3, 10-0, and 12-0 in their three victories in the Series. They pounded 13 more hits in the final game, which they tied by scoring twice in the top of the ninth. Mazeroski quickly untied it by depositing Terry's second pitch of the bottom half of the inning over the left-field fence for the winning home run. Mazeroski was mobbed by teammates and fans at home plate. His big hit remains the only winning home run in the bottom of the ninth inning of a World Series Game Seven.

The 1960 Series marked the Yankees' 11th trip to the Fall Classic in 14 years. New York would return each of the next four seasons, too, winning two and losing two, before the dynasty fizzled (at least temporarily).

In 1961, the Yankees easily handled the N.L.-champion Reds in five games. The key blow came in the top of the ninth inning of Game Three in Cincinnati. With the Series tied at 1–1 and the game tied at 2–2, the Yankees' Roger Maris came to bat against the Reds' Bob Purkey. Maris, who set a Major League record with 61 home runs during the regular season, belted a solo shot that gave New York a 3–2 victory and the Series lead. The next day, Whitey Ford extended his shutout string to 32 innings in the World Series, breaking Babe Ruth's record, and the Yankees won 7–0. They closed out the Series with a 13–5 rout in Game Five.

New York had to work considerably harder to get past the Giants in seven games in the 1962 Series. San Francisco, which had moved from New York only four years earlier,

earned its first trip to the World Series with a dramatic comeback victory in the ninth inning of the finale of a three-game playoff against the Dodgers. (It came 11 years to the day of Bobby Thomson's famous home run in 1951.)

■ *The 1966 Orioles' championship ring.*

The Yankees won Game One in San Francisco, then the teams traded victories until the Series was tied at three games each heading into the finale at Candlestick Park. Because rain delays in San Francisco meant there were five days between Games Five and Six, both teams were able to throw their aces in the finale: Ralph Terry for New York and Jack Sanford for the Giants. Terry fired a four-hitter to win 1–0. He survived when Bobby Richardson snagged Willie McCovey's wicked liner with runners on second and third for the final out in the Series.

The tables turned on New York in 1963, when it was the Yankees who were the victims of a masterful pitching performance. That year, left-hander Sandy Koufax and right-hander Don Drysdale helped the Dodgers to a four-game sweep. Koufax won Games One and Four, while Drysdale tossed a three-hit shutout in Game Three.

World Series 1960-1969: Arms Race, *continued*

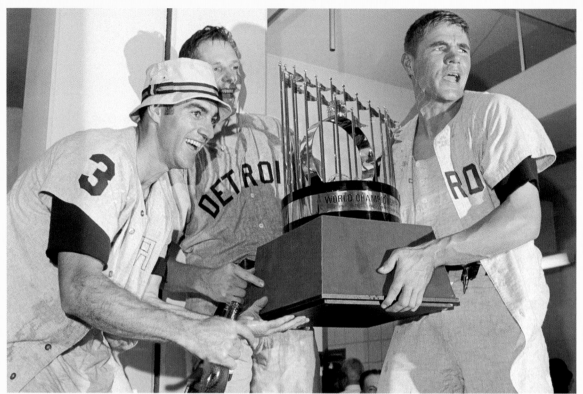

■ *With a thrilling victory in 1968, the Tigers earned the right to hoist the World Series trophy.*

In 1964, it was Cardinals ace Bob Gibson's turn to thwart the Yankees' title hopes. Gibson got the ball in Game Seven in St. Louis. He wasn't as dominant as he was during a 5–2 victory in 10 innings in Game Five, when he struck out 13 batters. But Gibson still fanned nine and went all the way in the Cardinals' 7–5 victory.

Gibson was back on the mound for Game Seven against the Boston Red Sox in 1967. He not only struck out 10 in that one, but he also hit a home run to help break open a 7–2 win at Fenway Park.

The next season, "Hoot" turned in one of the greatest pitching performances in baseball history. He went 22-9 with 13 shutouts and an ERA of 1.12. But after winning Games One and Four in the World Series against Detroit, he failed to nail down his third Game Seven of the decade. Detroit broke a scoreless tie in the seventh inning and went on to win 4–1 behind Mickey Lolich's third win of the Fall Classic.

Lolich had a masterful Series, but the star left-hander of the decade was the Dodgers' Koufax. The Series MVP in 1963, he did it again in 1965. After pitching a four-hit shutout to beat the Twins 7–0 in Game Five that year, he came back on two days' rest to blank Minnesota 2–0 on only three hits in Game Seven.

The Dodgers themselves fell to an amazing exhibition of pitching in 1966. In the bottom of the third inning of Game One against the Orioles in Los Angeles, the Dodgers drew four walks to push across their second run of the game (the first came on a home run by Jim Lefebvre in the second inning.) Los Angeles would not score again the rest of the Series. Moe Drabowsky shut them down the rest of the way in a 5–2 victory in Game

One. Then, in succession, Jim Palmer, Wally Bunker, and Dave McNally tossed complete-game shutouts to close out Baltimore's four-game sweep. Outfielder Frank Robinson was the Series MVP for hitting a pair of key homers, though, including a fourth-inning blasted for the only run of the finale.

Three years later, the Orioles were heavily favored over a young National League team from New York, but the "Amazin' Mets" won in five games. After seven seasons of finishing no higher than ninth place in the 10-team National League, the Mets were World Series champs in just their eighth season of existence.

■ *The '69 Mets were amazin'.*

YEAR	WINNING TEAM	LOSING TEAM	RESULT (GAMES)	MOST VALUABLE PLAYER
1960	Pittsburgh Pirates	New York Yankees	4–3	Bobby Richardson, 2B, New York
1961	New York Yankees	Cincinnati Reds	4–1	Whitey Ford, P, New York
1962	New York Yankees	San Francisco Giants	4–3	Ralph Terry, P, New York
1963	Los Angeles Dodgers	New York Yankees	4–0	Sandy Koufax, P, Los Angeles
1964	St. Louis Cardinals	New York Yankees	4–3	Bob Gibson, P, St. Louis
1965	Los Angeles Dodgers	Minnesota Twins	4–3	Sandy Koufax, P, Los Angeles
1966	Baltimore Orioles	Los Angeles Dodgers	4–0	Frank Robinson, OF, Baltimore
1967	St. Louis Cardinals	Boston Red Sox	4–3	Bob Gibson, P, St. Louis
1968	Detroit Tigers	St. Louis Cardinals	4–3	Mickey Lolich, P, Detroit
1969	New York Mets	Baltimore Orioles	4–1	Donn Clendenon, 1B, New York

World Series 1970-1979: Green and Gold and Red

The Oakland Athletics, who were as colorful off the field as their green-and-gold jerseys were on the field, and the Cincinnati Reds were the dominant teams of the 1970s. But the decade also marked the return of the mighty New York Yankees after 14 seasons without a championship.

■ *Roberto Clemente (21) played best in big games.*

The Yankees had been the only Major League franchise to win three World Series in a row (they had strings of four straight from 1936–39 and five straight from 1949–1953) before the Oakland Athletics did it beginning in 1972. That year, they beat the Reds in seven games in a tight series in which six games were decided by one run.

Unheralded catcher Gene Tenace, who hit only .225 with 5 home runs in 227 at-bats during the regular season, made World Series history in Game One. He became the first player ever to hit home runs in each of his first two career Series at-bats. Both blasts came off the Reds' Gary Nolan, and they provided all the runs in Oakland's 3–2 victory. Tenace would go on to hit .348 with 4 homers and 9 RBI to earn Series MVP honors.

The turning point in the Series, though, came in Game Four at Oakland. The Athletics—or A's, as they were more commonly known under wild-and-crazy owner Charles O. Finley—were leading two games to one, but trailed to 2–1 entering their final turn at bat. Then, four consecutive singles (including one by Tenace) brought home two runs and gave Oakland a three-games-to-one lead.

Cincinnati battled back to win Games Five and Six, but Catfish Hunter, normally a starting pitcher, won the finale 3–2 while appearing in relief on only one day of rest.

Oakland beat the New York Mets in another seven-game Series in 1973. Hunter turned in the key pitching performance again after the A's returned to Oakland for Game Six trailing three games to two. He tossed 7.1 innings of one-run ball in a 3–1 victory that forced a deciding Game Seven.

In the finale, light-hitting shortstop Bert Campaneris and big-hitting outfielder Reggie Jackson slammed two-run homers in a four-run third inning off New York starter Jon Matlack. The A's went on to post a 5–2 victory. Reliever Darold Knowles got the final out in the Series by getting the Mets' Wayne Garrett to pop out with two men on base. Knowles became the first man to pitch in every game of a seven-game Fall Classic. But the big star was Jackson, who was making a name for himself as a big-game performer. He drove in six runs while batting .310 to earn Series MVP honors.

Oakland's five-game victory over the Dodgers in 1974 was more workmanlike than its taut wins in '72 and '73. All the games were close, but the A's won three straight in

■ *Boston won a 1975 game on Fisk's homer.*

Oakland after splitting Games One and Two in Los Angeles. A's pitchers allowed only 11 runs the entire Series. Reliever Rollie Fingers won one and saved two of Oakland's four victories while compiling a 1.93 ERA. After Joe Rudi broke a tie game in the seventh inning of Game Five with a solo home run, Fingers got the last six outs to nail down a 3–2 win for the A's.

Meanwhile, the "Big Red Machine" was warming up in Cincinnati. The Reds were victimized by third-baseman Brooks Robinson's brilliant fielding in 1970, when the Baltimore Orioles won in five games, and then by the A's in 1972. But in 1975, Cincinnati put it all

World Series 1970-1979: Green and Gold and Red, *continued*

■ *Mr. October: Reggie Jackson homered on three consecutive swings of the bat.*

together. Behind a lineup loaded with future Hall-of-Famers such as catcher Johnny Bench, first baseman Tony Perez, and second baseman Joe Morgan, the Reds won 108 games during the regular season and swept the Pittsburgh Pirates in the National League Championship Series. In the World Series, they outlasted the A.L.-champion Boston Red Sox in seven games in perhaps the greatest World Series ever.

Trailing three games to two, Boston held off elimination in Game Six when Bernie Carbo slugged a pinch-hit, three-run home-run in the bottom of the eighth inning at Fenway Park. Boston then forced Game Seven on Carlton Fisk's dramatic solo shot in the 12th. But Red Sox fans' hopes were dashed when the Reds rallied from a three-run deficit the next night to win 4–3 on Morgan's ninth-inning single.

The next year, Cincinnati was not challenged: 102 wins during the regular season, then seven in a row in the postseason. The last four came over the Yankees, as Bench hit .533 with a pair of home runs.

New York was making its first trip to the World Series since 1964. After falling short against the Reds, the Yankees went out and signed Jackson, the former A's star. Jackson stirred up controversy in New York, where he feuded with teammates and on-again, off-again manager Billy Martin. But he also inspired the "Bronx Zoo" to back-to-back World Series titles in 1977 and '78. Both wins came over the Dodgers, who fell in each of their three trips to the Series in the 1970s.

The signature game of Jackson's Hall-of-Fame career came in the sixth, and final, game of 1977. With the Yankees trailing 3–2 in the fourth inning, he came to bat against Los Angeles starter Burt Hooton and drilled a line drive over the fence in right field for a two-run home run that gave the Yankees the lead for good. The next inning, Jackson came up against reliever Elias Sosa, again with one on. On the first pitch, he hit a home run over the right-field wall. The next time up, Jack-

son led off the eighth against Charlie Hough. Again on the first pitch, Jackson hit a majestic home run to center field—three home runs on three consecutive swings off three different pitchers. New York won in a rout, 8–4.

The Pirates joined the A's, Reds, and Yankees as multiple World Series champs in the 1970s, although Pittsburgh's titles came at opposite ends of the decade. The Pirates downed the Baltimore Orioles in seven games in 1971 behind Roberto Clemente's clutch hitting. They victimized the Orioles again in seven games in '79. "We Are Family" was Pittsburgh's theme that season, with first baseman Wilbur "Pops" Stargell leading the way. The big slugger hit .400 with three home runs against the Orioles, including the go-ahead, two-run shot in a 4–1 victory in Game Seven.

YEAR	WINNING TEAM	LOSING TEAM	RESULT (GAMES)	MOST VALUABLE PLAYER
1970	Baltimore Orioles	Cincinnati Reds	4–1	Brooks Robinson, 3B, Baltimore
1971	Pittsburgh Pirates	Baltimore Orioles	4–3	Roberto Clemente, OF, Pittsburgh
1972	Oakland Athletics	Cincinnati Reds	4–3	Gene Tenace, C, Oakland
1973	Oakland Athletics	New York Mets	4–3	Reggie Jackson, OF, Oakland
1974	Oakland Athletics	Los Angeles Dodgers	4–1	Rollie Fingers, P, Oakland
1975	Cincinnati Reds	Boston Red Sox	4–3	Pete Rose, 3B, Cincinnati
1976	Cincinnati Reds	New York Yankees	4–0	Johnny Bench, C, Cincinnati
1977	New York Yankees	Los Angeles Dodgers	4–2	Reggie Jackson, OF, New York
1978	New York Yankees	Los Angeles Dodgers	4–2	Bucky Dent, SS, New York
1979	Pittsburgh Pirates	Baltimore Orioles	4–3	Willie Stargell, 1B, Pittsburgh

World Series 1980-1989: Spread the Wealth

The 1970s was the decade of the dynasty. Only eight different franchises made it to the World Series, and only five different clubs won it. But in the 1980s, Major League Baseball spread the wealth: 14 clubs reached the Fall Classic during the decade, and nine different clubs won it. One of them was the Philadelphia Phillies, who reached the top of the baseball world for the first (and still only) time in their long history.

The Phillies opened the decade with their watershed championship. Philadelphia's history dates to the early days of the National League, in 1883. (The league began in 1876.) The Phillies had only a pair of National League pennants to their credit, and they lost both the 1915 and 1950 World Series. In the late 1970s, though, manager Danny Ozark built a strong squad around third baseman Mike Schmidt and pitcher Steve Carlton. Philadelphia won three consecutive division titles beginning in 1976, but lost in the playoffs each time. By 1980, Ozark had given way to Dallas Green, and Philadelphia followed up another division title with a thrilling five-game victory over Houston in the National League Championship Series.

In the World Series, the Phillies and the Kansas City Royals went toe-to-toe in six close games. With the Series tied at two games each, Schmidt's single sparked a two-run, ninth-inning rally that gave Philadelphia a 4–3 victory in Game Five. Two nights later, Schmidt had the key two-run single in a 4–1 victory. Reliever Tug McGraw, who wriggled

■ *McGraw jumped for joy after Philly won.*

out of bases-loaded jams in each of the final two games, flung his glove high into the air after striking out Willie Wilson in Game Six to give the Phillies the first championship in their 97 years.

It hadn't been nearly so long for the Dodgers, who snapped a 16-year drought the next season. Los Angeles won the World Series in 1965, then lost four consecutive trips to the Fall Classic. The last two (1977 and 1978) came against the Yankees, but the Dodgers avenged

■ *The Padres couldn't get past the powerful Tigers in 1984.*

those defeats with a six-game victory over New York in 1981. Los Angeles dropped the first two games in the Series, then roared back to win four straight. The first three were one-run decisions, but the finale wasn't close: a 9–2 rout over former Dodger left-hander Tommy John.

Los Angeles, which also beat the Oakland Athletics in 1988, was the only team to win the World Series twice in the 1980s. The '88 Series produced one of the most dramatic moments in baseball history.

The Dodgers were heavy underdogs heading into the Series against the Athletics, who were dominant en route to 104 victories

during the regular season. Plus, Los Angeles looked as if it might have to play without injured Kirk Gibson, the fiery outfielder who was the National League's MVP that season.

Behind Jose Canseco's second-inning grand slam, Oakland took a 4–3 lead into the bottom of the ninth inning of Game One. The Athletics called on relief ace Dennis Eckersley, who had saved a Major League-leading 45 games that year. Eckersley got the first two outs of the ninth, but then walked pinch-hitter Mike Davis.

Then Gibson hobbled out of the dugout, injured legs and all. It would turn out to be his lone at-bat of the Series—but what an

World Series 1980-1989: Spread the Wealth, *continued*

at-bat it was! Gibson quickly fell behind two strikes, then worked the count to three balls and two strikes. Eckersley tried to put a slider on the outside corner of the plate, but Gibson muscled an improbable home run over the right-field wall that gave Los Angeles a 5–4 victory and sparked a five-game upset.

■ *Gibson: one of baseball's most dramatic moments.*

Gibson was on the field a lot more for the 1984 World Series, when he was with the Detroit Tigers. "Gibby" hit .333 in an easy, five-game victory over the San Diego Padres. He belted a pair of home runs in an 8–4 victory in the finale, with the second reaching the upper deck at Tiger Stadium. He punctuated his home-run trot with an emphatic stomp on home plate.

In addition to Gibson's heroics, there were several memorable World Series moments in the 1980s. In 1985, the St. Louis Cardinals were three outs away from their second title of the decade before a blown call at first base opened the doors for the Royals to win Game Six. The next night, Kansas City roared to an 11–0 victory.

The following year, it was the Boston Red Sox who were on the verge of a Series-ending win in Game Six. Boston, which was looking for its first World Series championship since 1918, scored two times in the top of the 10th inning to take a 5–3 lead against the New York Mets. In the home half of the inning, the first two Mets were down to their last out before rallying for three runs. The game-winning score came when Mookie Wilson's slow grounder slipped through first baseman Bill Buckner's legs for an error. New York won the game 6–5. The Mets' 8–5 win in Game Seven the next evening extended Boston's agonizing World Series drought.

In 1987, the Minnesota Twins outlasted the St. Louis Cardinals in seven games. Kent Hrbek's key grand slam in the sixth inning of Game Six was the big blow.

Oakland beat Bay Area-rival San Francisco in 1989. But the Series is remembered less for the Athletics' easy victory than for a devastating earthquake that struck the region as the teams were preparing to take the field for Game Three at Candlestick Park. Oakland was up two games at the time; after a 10-day delay, the Athletics won the final two games.

■ *Hrbek celebrates his 1987 Series grand slam.*

YEAR	WINNING TEAM	LOSING TEAM	RESULT (GAMES)	MOST VALUABLE PLAYER
1980	Philadelphia Phillies	Kansas City Royals	4–2	Mike Schmidt, 3B, Philadelphia
1981	Los Angeles Dodgers	New York Yankees	4–2	Ron Cey, 3B, Los Angeles Pedro Guerrero, OF, Los Angeles Steve Yeager, C, Los Angeles
1982	St. Louis Cardinals	Milwaukee Brewers	4–3	Darrell Porter, C, St. Louis
1983	Baltimore Orioles	Philadelphia Phillies	4–1	Rick Dempsey, C, Baltimore
1984	Detroit Tigers	San Diego Padres	4–1	Alan Trammell, SS, Detroit
1985	Kansas City Royals	St. Louis Cardinals	4–3	Bret Saberhagen, P, Kansas City
1986	New York Mets	Boston Red Sox	4–3	Ray Knight, 3B, New York
1987	Minnesota Twins	St. Louis Cardinals	4–3	Frank Viola, P, Minnesota
1988	Los Angeles Dodgers	Oakland Athletics	4–1	Orel Hershiser, P, Los Angeles
1989	Oakland Athletics	San Francisco Giants	4–0	Dave Stewart, P, Oakland

World Series 1990–1999: Pardon the Interruption

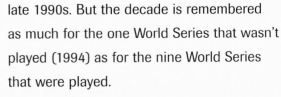

After the New York Yankees' longest World Series drought (14 seasons without an appearance) and championship drought (18 years without winning) since they first appeared in the Fall Classic in 1921, the franchise returned to dynasty level in the

■ *Hometown hero Jack Morris starred in 1991.*

late 1990s. But the decade is remembered as much for the one World Series that wasn't played (1994) as for the nine World Series that were played.

The 1994 season was shaping up to be a banner year. San Diego's Tony Gwynn flirted with a .400 batting average. (He hit .394.) San Francisco's Matt Williams and Seattle's Ken Griffey Jr. each threatened Babe Ruth's single-season home-run record. (Williams had 43 round-trippers with more than six weeks still to play on the regular schedule, and Griffey had 40.) Jeff Bagwell drove in 116 runs in Houston's 115 games.

But on August 12 of that year, Major League players decided to strike. They were arguing with owners about a variety of labor issues. Soon, the rest of the regular season and all of the playoffs were cancelled. For the first time since 1904, when the N.L.-champion New York Giants refused to play the A.L.-champion Boston Red Sox, the World Series was not played.

The players' strike ended the Toronto Blue Jays' two-year run as

World Series champs. The Blue Jays' second title came in dramatic fashion, when Joe Carter blasted a one-out, three-run home run in the bottom of the ninth inning to give his team an 8–6 victory over Philadelphia in the deciding Game Six in 1993. It was the first Series walk-off homer since Pittsburgh's Bill Mazeroski in 1960.

■ *A labor disagreement kept ballparks empty at 1994 Series time.*

The season before, Toronto had become the first team outside the United States to win the World Series. The Blue Jays beat the Braves in six games that year, winning the finale 4–3 in 11 innings.

The Cincinnati Reds opened the decade with a stunning four-game sweep of Oakland. The Athletics, who were making their third consecutive trip to the Fall Classic, were heavily favored. Not only did the defending champs win 103 games during the regular season, but they also entered the World Series with a 10-game postseason winning streak dating to the 1989 American League Championship Series. Oakland featured the hitting of the "Bash Brothers," Mark McGwire and Jose Canseco, the baserunning of Rickey Henderson, and the pitching of 27-game winner Bob Welch.

In the opener, though, right-hander Jose Rijo combined with two relievers on a 7–0 shutout in Cincinnati. The Reds took the next two games, too, and carried a 2–1 lead behind Rijo into the bottom of the ninth inning of Game Four. With one out, Randy Myers came on to get Canseco to ground out and Carney Lansford to foul out, ending the game and the Series.

Cincinnati did not return to the Fall Classic the rest of the decade, however (and has not been back at all since). Instead, Atlanta was the National League's dominant team of the 1990s, winning a division title each season (except 1994, when there were no official division winners) and taking the pennant five times. But the Braves struggled mightily in the World Series, losing four times, including

World Series 1990-1999: Pardon the Interruption, *continued*

a gut-wrenching, seven-game decision to the Minnesota Twins in 1991. In that Series, the home team won every game. The Twins got it started by taking a pair of close decisions at their noisy stadium, the Hubert H. Humphrey Metrodome, in Games One and Two.

In Atlanta, the Braves countered by eking out a pair of one-run contests in their final at-bat in Games Three and Four before pounding out a 14–5 victory in Game Five.

But then it was back to the Metrodome for the final two games. In Game Six, out-

■ *Steinbrenner (left) and Torre: tears of joy.*

fielder Kirby Puckett made a leaping catch at the wall during a game that went extra innings tied at 3–3. In the 11th inning, he won it with a home run. The next night, the Twins' Jack Morris (who was born in St. Paul, Minnesota) and the Braves' John Smoltz locked in one of the great pitching duels in World Series history.

Smoltz did not allow a run in 7.1 innings before giving way to relievers Mike Stanton and Alejandro Pena. Morris was even better. He went 10 innings, allowing only seven hits and no runs, and striking out eight. In the bottom of the 10th, Minnesota's Gene Larkin drove home Dan Gladden with a sacrifice fly for the winning run.

Atlanta's lone World Series win came in 1995. That year, the Braves bested the Cleveland Indians in a tight six-game Series. All of the games were close (five of them were decided by one run). In the finale, Dave Justice homered for the game's only run, and Tom Glavine and Mark Wohlers combined on a one-hit shutout.

The Indians were denied their first World Series triumph since 1948 that year, then again two seasons later. It was the Florida Marlins who did it in dramatic fashion in 1997. Cleveland led 2–0 in Game Seven before Florida scored one run in the seventh, one run in the ninth, and one run in the 11th—on a bases-loaded single by Edgar Renteria—to win. Surprisingly, the Marlins were in only their fifth season of existence.

Owner George Steinbrenner's Yankees, who had been around considerably longer, played in the World Series in 1996 for the first time since 1981. Their six-game victory over the Braves marked their first title since 1978. But New York was just getting started. Manager Joe Torre's 1998 team won a club-record 114 games during the regular season, and swept the overmatched San Diego Padres in four games in the World Series.

The next year, it was the Braves who went down in four games to the Yankees. New York closer Mariano Riverawon one game and saved two others.

■ *Renteria celebrated the Marlins' victory.*

YEAR	WINNING TEAM	LOSING TEAM	RESULT (GAMES)	MOST VALUABLE PLAYER
1990	Cincinnati Reds	Oakland Athletics	4–0	Jose Rijo, P, Cincinnati
1991	Minnesota Twins	Atlanta Braves	4–3	Jack Morris, P, Minnesota
1992	Toronto Blue Jays	Atlanta Braves	4–2	Pat Borders, C, Toronto
1993	Toronto Blue Jays	Philadelphia Phillies	4–2	Paul Molitor, DH-1B-3B, Toronto
1994	World Series not played			
1995	Atlanta Braves	Cleveland Indians	4–2	Tom Glavine, P, Atlanta
1996	New York Yankees	Atlanta Braves	4–2	John Wetteland, P, New York
1997	Florida Marlins	Cleveland Indians	4–3	Livan Hernandez, P, Florida
1998	New York Yankees	San Diego Padres	4–0	Scott Brosius, 3B, New York
1999	New York Yankees	Atlanta Braves	4–0	Mariano Rivera, P, New York

World Series 2000s: A Curse Reversed

The 2000s opened the same way that the 1990s closed—with the New York Yankees winning the World Series. But it was hardly business as usual after that, with new champions Arizona, Anaheim, and Florida winning titles before the Boston Red Sox finally ended many decades of frustration with a sweep of the St. Louis Cardinals in 2004.

■ *The city celebrated the Yankees' 2000 title.*

The Yankees' victory over the New York Mets in a "Subway Series" in 2000 marked their third championship in a row. Three or more World Series championships had been accomplished only four times in baseball history; three of those times, it was by the Yankees (the other time was by the Oakland Athletics during the 1970s). New York's bid for a fourth straight title, though, was ended by the Diamondbacks in 2001. The Yankees led Game Seven 2-1 and had Mariano Rivera—a previously untouchable closer in World Series play—on the mound in the ninth inning. Arizona rallied for two runs, though, with the game-winner scoring on Luis Gonzalez' soft single into left-center field. The Diamondbacks won a World Series faster than any other expansion franchise in history. It was only their fourth season.

The Angels had been around since 1961, but they entered the 2002 Fall Classic looking for their first title, too. Behind sluggers Barry Bonds (who hit .471 with four home runs in the Series) and Jeff Kent (who hit three homers), the Giants took a three-games-to-two lead into Game Six in Anaheim.

San Francisco took a 5-0 lead into the bottom of the seventh inning, and it looked as if the Giants would win their first title since 1954, when the club was still in New York. But Anaheim forged an historic rally. No team ever had come from five runs down while facing elimination until the Angels got three runs in the seventh and three in the eighth to win Game Six 6–5. The next night, Anaheim took Game Seven 4–1 behind rookie starting pitcher John Lackey.

The Yankees were back in the World Series for the sixth time in eight years in 2003, but the Florida Marlins pulled off an upset in six games. MVP Josh Beckett won the finale 2–0 by tossing a five-hit gem. The young Marlins won a World Series for the second time in only 11 seasons as a big-league franchise.

The story of the decade, though, was the Red Sox, who won the World Series in 2004 and 2007. One of baseball's best teams of the early 20th century, Boston

■ *Roberts and the Red Sox were on top of the world in 2004.*

World Series 2000s: A Curse Reversed, *continued*

won the World Series five times from 1903 (the birth of the modern Fall Classic) through 1918. After the 1919 season, though, the Red Sox sold Babe Ruth to the rival Yankees. New York went on to become big-league baseball's dominant franchise, while Boston did not win another championship through 2003. The heartbreaking fashion in which the Red Sox often lost was blamed on the "Curse of the Bambino."

The curse appeared to be alive and well when the Red Sox couldn't protect a three-run lead against the rival Yankees in the bottom of the eighth inning of Game Seven of the 2003 American League Championship Series, and eventually lost in 11 innings.

Then, in 2004, Boston and New York squared off again in the ALCS. The Red Sox dropped the first three games of the series. They came from behind late in Games Four and Five, though, then beat New York at Yankee Stadium in Games Six and Seven to reach the Fall Classic.

The World Series against the Cardinals was almost anticlimactic. St. Louis won 105 games during the regular season, but never had a chance against Boston, which didn't trail in any game. Outfielder Manny Ramirez batted .412, while Curt Schilling, Pedro Martinez, and Derek Lowe turned in masterful pitching performances.

Just to prove that their first championship in 86 years was no fluke, the Red Sox won again three years later. The Colorado Rockies, who entered their first World Series with 21 wins in 22 games (including playoffs), fell in four straight.

The Red Sox' sweeps were sandwiched around another pair of lopsided World Series. In 2005, the Chicago White Sox swept the Houston Astros. In that Series, another Sox ended another long string of Series losses.

■ *The Chicago White Sox ended a long drought in 2005.*

Chicago's previous triumph had been all the way back in 1917; they hadn't even made it to the Fall Classic since 1959. Chicago was led in 2005 by the slugging of outfielder Jermaine Dye and first baseman Paul Konerko and the pitching of lefty Mark Buehrle.

In 2006, the St. Louis Cardinals needed only five games to beat the Detroit Tigers. The Cardinals' title was their 10th, putting them second only to the Yankees' 26 wins in the Fall Classic. The Cardinals' 83 wins in the regular season were the fewest ever for a World Series champ.

■ *The Rockies were no match for the Red Sox in '07.*

The 2008 World Series featured some wild weather. The Tampa Bay Rays made the Series after having the league's worst record a year earlier. With the Philadelphia Phillies ahead three games to one, rain forced the first suspended game in Series history. Two days later, the teams met again and picked up where they left off. The Phillies won that game and the Series, only their second ever.

YEAR	WINNING TEAM	LOSING TEAM	RESULT (GAMES)	MOST VALUABLE PLAYER
2000	New York Yankees	New York Mets	4–1	Derek Jeter, SS, New York
2001	Arizona Diamondbacks	New York Yankees	4–3	Randy Johnson, P, Arizona Curt Schilling, P, Arizona
2002	Anaheim Angels	San Francisco Giants	4–3	Troy Glaus, 3B, Anaheim
2003	Florida Marlins	New York Yankees	4–2	Josh Beckett, P, Florida
2004	Boston Red Sox	St. Louis Cardinals	4–0	Manny Ramirez, OF, Boston
2005	Chicago White Sox	Houston Astros	4–0	Jermaine Dye, OF, Chicago
2006	St. Louis Cardinals	Detroit Tigers	4–1	David Eckstein, SS, St. Louis
2007	Boston Red Sox	Colorado Rockies	4–0	Mike Lowell, 3B, Boston
2008	Philadelphia Phillies	Tampa Bay Rays	4-1	Cole Hamels, P, Philadelphia

World War I and Baseball

In 1917, World War I was almost three years old when the United States finally entered the conflict. Millions of young men were drafted into the Army and sent to Europe to fight. Baseball players were no exception. More than 250 signed up to serve, including stars such as Christy Mathewson. The 1917 season was not affected much, though many players left and attendance dipped. In 1918, the U.S. government decided that baseball could continue, but that the season would end at Labor Day.

Two changes to the game came out of war-related issues: For the first time, Sunday baseball was played at all stadiums. Some cities had not allowed it before then due to religious objections. And "The Star-Spangled Banner" was played before all games during the war, a practice that soon became standard for games at all levels.

■ *Ballplayer-turned-soldier Christy Mathewson.*

World War II and Baseball

In 1939, another war started in Europe. Detroit first baseman Hank Greenberg was one of just a few ballplayers to join up at that early stage. However, the United States was still not officially in the war. By the end of 1941, however, America had joined the fight. Bob Feller, star pitcher of the Indians, signed up to fight a month after Pearl Harbor (December 7, 1941). Ted Williams left for the Navy by June, 1942. Joe DiMaggio and others signed up, too, and played on service teams. The key event for baseball was the famous "Green-Light Letter" sent by President Roosevelt to Commissioner Kenesaw Landis. In the letter, Roosevelt said that he felt baseball should continue during the war to help people back home and give workers a break from making the tools of war. So baseball played on, though at a lower level of quality due to the missing players.

■ *Indians ace Bob Feller (second from left) pitched for a Navy team during part of World War II.*

When the war ended in 1945, most players returned to their teams. However, some of them, such as Williams and Greenberg, had given up some of the prime years of their career to fight for their country.

Wright, David

Wright's combination of speed and power have made him one of the top all-around players in the National League. A third baseman for the Mets since 2004,

Wright is a three-time All-Star and led the Mets to the playoffs in 2006. He joined the 30–30 Club (at least 30 steals and homers in the same season) in 2007.

Wright, George and Harry

The Wright brothers of airplane fame were not the first siblings with that name to gain national attention. George and Harry Wright, who originally were cricket stars, were among the top players in

■ *A 1869 photo of baseball pioneers Harry (top left) and George Wright (top right).*

founding the Reds, he also helped start the National Association, which later became the National League. He was the Reds' manager, too, and created many things that are a part of baseball today: backing up plays in the field, pregame fungo practice, the double steal, and the hidden-ball trick. Wright was also the first manager to have his players wear knickers, still a classic part of the official baseball uniform. He also emphasized sportsmanship in a game that was leaning toward too much unfair play.

While George made the Hall of Fame in 1937, Harry didn't join his brother there until 1953.

Wrigley Field

The oldest ballpark still in use in the National League, Wrigley Field is the home of the Chicago Cubs. They were not the park's first team, however. The ballpark was built in 1914 to hold the Chicago Whales of the newly formed Federal League. That league ended after two seasons, however, and the Cubs happily moved in for the 1916 season.

Wrigley is famous for several things. It has ivy growing on its brick outfield walls, and sometimes fielders lose the ball when it rolls into the ivy. It was the last ballpark with lights, not turning them on until 1988. In fact, most of its home games are still played during the day. And its fans are known as the "Bleacher Bums," always

early pro baseball and played a big part in the formation of the National League.

George Wright was already a top player when his brother Harry formed the first openly pro team in 1869, the Cincinnati Red Stockings. As a shortstop, George Wright had no equal, and he was among the top hitters in just about every league in which he played. Harry Wright, however, was a true baseball pioneer. Along with cheering for their beloved—if often losing—Cubbies and tossing enemy home-run balls back onto the field. Fans can also sit on nearby rooftops and look in on the game.

The area around Wrigley, in the middle of Chicago's North Side, is known as Wrigleyville and becomes a busy village of fans and visitors on game days.

Wynn, Early

For a guy named Early, it turned out that he had some of his greatest seasons late in his career. Wynn began his pro career in 1939 with the Washington Senators. They were mostly awful while he was with them, but he did win 18 games in 1943. After moving to Cleveland in 1949, he joined a staff that was among the American League's best in the 1950s. Wynn won 20 games three times with the Indians and helped them win the 1954 A.L. pennant.

In 1959, having moved to the White Sox a year earlier, Wynn had best season at the age of 39. He won 22 games, led the league in strikeouts, and won the Cy Young Award. The "old" man led the youthful "Go-Go" Sox into the World Series, but they lost to the Dodgers.

Wynn reached exactly 300 wins with his final career victory in 1963 in a short stint back with Cleveland. He was elected to the Hall of Fame in 1972.

This well-known sign greets visitors to Chicago's Wrigley Field, one of America's oldest ballparks.

■ *Yankees fans across the nation were sad when Yankee Stadium closed after the 2008 season.*

Yankee Stadium

The home of the Yankees from 1923 through 2008, Yankee Stadium was closed and torn down to make way for a new Yankee Stadium that opened in 2009. But the old place still lives on in baseball memory as the home to many of baseball's greatest heroes and most famous moments.

The ballpark became known as "The House That Ruth Built" because Babe Ruth was a star for the Yankees in 1923. In fact, he hit the first homer in the stadium on Opening Day, 1923. The Yankees won the World Series that year, the first of 26 they would win through 2008. Yankee Stadium was the first triple-deck, big-league ballpark, seating more than 50,000 fans.

Among its famous distinctions was Monument Park. The first on-field monument was to manager Miller Huggins, who died in 1932. Lou Gehrig got one in 1941 after his death, and Ruth was honored with one in 1948. The three stone tablets were actually on the playing field until 1976, when they were moved behind the fences in left field. Many other memorials or plaques were added over the years to honor Yankee greats and events at the park, such as Masses said by Pope Paul VI (1965) and Pope John Paul II (1979).

Yastrzemski, Carl

Taking over for a legend is never easy, but Carl Yastrzemski not only took over for one, he became one. "Yaz" stepped into the shoes and left-field position of Red Sox star Ted Williams in 1961. By 1963, the hard-working left-handed batter had won the first of three A.L. batting titles. Yaz also was becoming one of the best defensive outfielders in the game. He would win seven Gold Gloves and lead the American League in assists seven times.

In 1967, Yaz had one of the greatest seasons in recent decades. Not only did he win the Triple Crown (leading the league in homers, RBI, and batting average), but he also carried a Red Sox team that had finished eighth in 1966 into the World Series. "The Impossible Dream" is still remembered fondly all over New England. Yaz went 7–for–8 in the last two games, and Boston won the pennant on the last day. Though the Red Sox lost to the Cardinals in the World Series in seven games, Yaz had 2 homers and 7 RBI.

He won another batting title in 1968 and missed a fourth in 1970 by a whisker. He helped the Red Sox win another title in 1975. In 1978, he was, sadly, the last out in a famous single-game playoff with the Yankees for the A.L. East title. But the next year, he became the first A.L. player ever to reach both 400 homers and 3,000 hits for his career. When he retired in 1983, he ran all around Fenway Park, exchanging high fives with the fans who had loved him for 23 years. His time with the Red Sox is tied with Brooks Robinson of the Orioles for the longest service ever with one club. Yaz was never the flashiest player or the smoothest, but he played hard, he won, and he was a leader. He was elected to the Hall of Fame in 1989. Fans had never forgotten Williams, but they also had another hero to remember in Yaz.

■ *Yaz won the A.L. Triple Crown in 1967.*

■ *Young's records may never be broken.*

Yankee Stadium underwent a major renovation in 1975, and the Yankees played at Shea Stadium for two years. But they won a World Series in 1977, their first year back "home," mirroring the 1923 opening. By 2006, however, the stadium was getting old, and the team and the city (the co-owners) decided to build a new, modern ballpark in the same neighborhood. The new Yankee Stadium still has Monument Park and recalls many of the same details as the old place.

Young, Cy

You don't get a major award named after you without putting up some pretty amazing numbers. Cy Young's career mark of 511 wins is universally regarded as an unbreakable record. No pitcher in the past 75 years has come within 150 wins of the great right-hander.

His real name was Denton True Young. He got his nickname either from his farming background (Cy was a name often given to young farmers) or from his ability to throw like a cyclone. Young started his career in 1890 with the Cleveland Spiders of the National League. He won at least 20 games for them in nine straight years, including a career high of 36 wins in 1892. After moving to Boston of the American League in 1901, he just kept rolling, with four seasons of more than 25 wins. He had 28 wins in 1903 as he helped Boston, then known as the Americans, win the first World Series. The next year, he threw a first perfect game at the age of 37.

He was not an overpowering pitcher, never leading the league in strikeouts, but he was an overall outstanding hurler. By the time he retired in 1911, he had put the wins mark out of reach. He also, it should be noted, put the losses mark out there, too: Young lost a record 316 games.

He was named as one of the members of the second class of the Hall of Fame in 1937. The award for the top pitcher in each league was named for him in 1956.

Yount, Robin

A multitalented player, Robin Yount is one of only three players in history to win a league MVP award at two different positions. He won it in 1982 while playing shortstop and in 1989 while playing center field. Yount played his entire 20-year career with the Milwaukee Brewers, beginning as an 18-year-old phenom in 1974. He was neither a huge slugger nor a batting champ, but he was always a high-level producer, while also helping out on the bases (he stole at least 15 bases in eight different seasons). Yount helped the "Brew Crew" win the 1982 A.L. pennant and batted .414 in Milwaukee's losing World Series effort.

The three-time All-Star finished with 3,142 hits and was elected to the Hall of Fame in 1999.

■ *Yount played two positions at All-Star levels.*

Zito, Barry

It's not over yet, but through 2008, Barry Zito's place in history might be that he was one of the worst free-agent signings ever. Zito was the A.L. Rookie of the Year in 2001, when he won 17 games for Oakland, and he followed that with a 23–5 season in 2003 that earned him the Cy Young Award. A three-time All-Star, he signed an enormous contract before the 2007 season to join the cross-Bay San Francisco Giants. The Giants will pay him about $125 million over seven years, but in his first two seasons there, he was just 21–30 with an ERA of 4.83.

The Best Baseball Song

In 1908, a new song hit the music halls of New York City and other towns. Albert Von Tilzer wrote the music for the song, while Jack Norworth wrote the words. The song soon became popular, especially among baseball fans. "Take Me Out to the Ball Game" has since become one of the best-known and most-sung songs of all time. It's sung during the seventh-inning stretch at nearly every ballpark at every level. Kids know it, grownups bellow it, and famous singers have recorded versions. But almost no one knows that the version everyone sings is just part of a longer song!

Katie Casey was base ball# mad.
Had the fever and had it bad;
Just to root for the home town crew,
Ev'ry sou* Katie blew.
On a Saturday, her young beau
Called to see if she'd like to go,
To see a show but Miss Kate said,
"No, I'll tell you what you can do."

"Take me out to the ball game,
Take me out with the crowd.
Buy me some peanuts and cracker jack**,
I don't care if I never get back,
Let me root, root, root for the home team***,
If they don't win it's a shame.
For it's one, two, three strikes, you're out,
At the old ball game."

Katie Casey saw all the games,
Knew the players by their first names;
Told the umpire he was wrong,
All along good and strong.
When the score was just two to two,
Katie Casey knew what to do,
Just to cheer up the boys she knew,
She made the gang sing this song:

"Take me out to the ball game,
Take me out with the crowd.
Buy me some peanuts and cracker jack,
I don't care if I never get back,
Let me root, root, root for the home team,
If they don't win it's a shame.
For it's one, two, three strikes, your out,
At the old ball game."

\# *In the early 1900s, many people still spelled the sport as two words, "base ball."*
* *A slang term for money*
** *In 2004, the Yankees tried to replace Cracker Jack with a similar snack food. Fans objected so much the team switched back!*
*** *Many fans swap in the name of their favorite team instead of singing "home team."*

Triple Crown Winners

It's one of baseball's rarest hitting feats. Winning the Triple Crown demands not only batting excellence, but also power and great timing. A Triple Crown winner leads his league in home runs, runs batted in, and batting average. How hard is it? Think of the great hitters of the past few decades—George Brett, Barry Bonds, Albert Pujols, Alex Rodriguez. None of these sluggers have won the Triple Crown. Here's a list of all the men who have earned this honor. Who do you think will be the next player we add to this list?

■ *Williams: two Triple Crowns.*

Year	Player, Team	HR	RBI	Avg.
1967	Carl Yastrzemski, Red Sox	44	121	.326
1966	Frank Robinson, Orioles	49	122	.316
1956	Mickey Mantle, Yankees	52	130	.353
1947	Ted Williams, Red Sox	32	114	.343
1942	Ted Williams, Red Sox	36	137	.356
1937	Joe Medwick, Cardinals	31	154	.374
1934	Lou Gehrig, Yankees	49	165	.363
1933	Jimmie Foxx, Athletics	48	163	.356
1933	Chuck Klein, Phillies	28	120	.368
1925	Rogers Hornsby, Cardinals	39	143	.403
1922	Rogers Hornsby, Cardinals	42	152	.401
1909	Ty Cobb, Tigers	9	107	.377
1901	Nap Lajoie, White Sox	14	125	.426
1894	Hugh Duffy, Boston	18	145	.440
1887	Tip O'Neill, St. Louis	14	123	.435
1878	Paul Hines, Providence	4	50	.358

Unassisted Triple Plays

Making an unassisted triple play demands three things: good glove work, quick thinking . . . and luck. There are only a few situations in which such a play can actually happen–first and second or bases loaded, either with no outs. The runners have to be moving on the pitch to make such a play, so you've got runners far from safe bases and near the fielder with the ball. All of these plays started with a line drive caught by a fielder, and all but two of them had the second out made at second base. Unassisted triple plays are exciting and extremely rare–but lucky fans saw one in both 2007 and 2008 . . . so watch carefully when the situations listed above come up!

■ *Three outs in one: Asdrubal Cabrera completes his 2008 triple play.*

Date	Player, Position, Team
May 12, 2008	Asdrubal Cabrera, 2B, Indians
April 29, 2007	Troy Tulowitzki, SS, Rockies
Aug. 10, 2003	Rafael Furcal, SS, Braves
May 29, 2000	Randy Velarde, 2B, Athletics
July 8, 1994	John Valentin, SS, Red Sox
Sept. 20, 1992	Mickey Morandini, 2B, Phillies
July 30, 1968	Ron Hansen, SS, Senators
May 31, 1927	Johnny Neun, 1B, Tigers
May 30, 1927	Jimmy Cooney, SS, Cubs
May 7, 1925	Glenn Wright, SS, Pirates
Oct. 6, 1923	Ernie Padgett, SS, Braves
Sept. 14, 1923	George Burns, 1B, Red Sox
Oct. 10, 1920	Bill Wambsganss, 2B, Indians
July 19, 1909	Neal Ball, SS, Indians

The Men in Blue

At every baseball game, there are three types of people on the field: players from one team, players from the other team, and umpires. At Major League games, four umpires work during regular-season games, and six work at postseason games. Just like players, umpires have to work their way up through the minors. The very best umpires make "the Show," and often keep their jobs for many years. Until 2000, each league hired its own umpires. Since that year, however, Major League Baseball now hires all umpires and assigns them to work games in either the American or the National League. Here are the Major League umpires for the 2008 season.

No.	Name	No.	Name	No.	Name	No.	Name
67	Lance Barksdale	60	Marty Foster	96	Paul Nauert	5	Dale Scott
65	Ted Barrett	53	Greg Gibson	45	Jeff Nelson	95	Tim Timmons
35	Wally Bell	9	Brian Gorman	7	Brian O'Nora	4	Tim Tschida
54	C.B. Bucknor	20	Tom Hallion	39	Larry Poncino	27	Larry Vanover
48	Mark Carlson	55	Angel Hernandez	59	Tony Randazzo	47	Mark Wegner
38	Gary Cederstrom	15	Ed Hickox	19	Ed Rapuano	52	Bill Welke
56	Eric Cooper	17	John Hirschbeck	23	Rick Reed	3	Tim Welke
13	Derryl Cousins	29	Bill Hohn	31	Mike Reilly	21	Hunter
2	Jerry Crawford	34	Sam Holbrook	18	Charlie Reliford		Wendelstedt
25	Fielding Culbreth	51	Marvin Hudson	77	Jim Reynolds	22	Joe West
10	Phil Cuzzi	58	Dan Iassogna	71	Brian Runge	33	Mike Winters
44	Kerwin Danley	66	Jim Joyce	43	Paul Schrieber	78	Jim Wolf
37	Gary Darling	8	Jeff Kellogg				
61	Bob Davidson	46	Ron Kulpa				
12	Gerry Davis	24	Jerry Layne				
32	Dana DeMuth	72	Alfonso Marquez				
63	Laz Diaz	30	Randy Marsh				
16	Mike DiMuro	36	Tim McClelland				
1	Bruce Dreckman	41	Jerry Meals				
88	Doug Eddings	14	Chuck				
50	Paul Emmel		Meriwether				
57	Mike Everitt	26	Bill Miller				
49	Andy Fletcher	11	Ed Montague				

Umpires in the Baseball Hall of Fame

Name	Year Inducted
Al Barlick	1989
Nestor Chylak	1999
Jocko Conlan	1974
Tom Connolly	1953
Billy Evans	1973
Cal Hubbard	1976
Bill Klem	1953
Bill McGowan	1992

Who's on First?

The most famous baseball comedy routine of all time was first performed by the team of Bud Abbott and Lou Costello in 1940. Costello played a new player trying to learn the names of his teammates. Abbott was the manager trying to fill him in. However, the nicknames of the players were so unusual that Costello became frustrated trying to learn them. Their back-and-forth chat has become a regular feature at ballparks. It plays almost constantly at a special display at the Baseball Hall of Fame. You can read the positions of the routine's "team" below, but until you hear the act for yourself . . . you won't really understand why it's so funny.

Position	Name
First base	Who
Second base	What
Third base	I Don't Know
Shortstop	I Don't Give a Darn
Left field	Why
Center field	Because
Right field	(not named)
Pitcher	Tomorrow
Catcher	Today

■ *Abbott (left) and Costello's routine was honored with this special baseball card.*

Women's Pro Baseball

While no woman has played Major League Baseball, women have played pro baseball. The first to do so took part in a league founded during World War II, when many men were away in military service. The teams, most located in the Midwest, played to crowds that were large to begin with, but numbers slowly shrank—especially after servicemen returned to refill Major-League rosters. In 1994, a women's pro team was formed by a beer company. The Silver Bullets played against men's amateur and pro teams, but the team lasted only three years. Here are the teams that took part in the All-American Girls' Professional Baseball League from 1943–54.

1943
Kenosha Comets
Racine Belles
Rockford Peaches
South Bend Blue Sox

1944
Kenosha Comets
Milwaukee Chicks
Minneapolis Millerettes
Racine Belles
Rockford Peaches
South Bend Blue Sox

1945
Fort Wayne Daisies
Grand Rapids Chicks
Kenosha Comets
Racine Belles
Rockford Peaches
South Bend Blue Sox

1946
Fort Wayne Daisies
Grand Rapids Chicks
Kenosha Comets
Muskegon Lassies
Peoria Redwings
Racine Belles
Rockford Peaches
South Bend Blue Sox

1947
Fort Wayne Daisies
Grand Rapids Chicks
Kenosha Comets
Muskegon Lassies
Peoria Redwings
Racine Belles
Rockford Peaches
South Bend Blue Sox

1948
Chicago Colleens
Fort Wayne Daisies
Grand Rapids Chicks
Kenosha Comets
Muskegon Lassies
Peoria Redwings
Racine Belles
Rockford Peaches
South Bend Blue Sox
Springfield Sallies

1949
Ft Wayne Daisies
Grand Rapids Chicks
Kenosha Comets
Muskegon Lassies
Peoria Redwings
Racine Belles
Rockford Peaches
South Bend Blue Sox

1950
Chicago Colleens
Ft Wayne Daisies
Grand Rapids Chicks
Kalamazoo Lassies
Kenosha Comets
Peoria Redwings
Racine Belles
Rockford Peaches
South Bend Blue Sox
Springfield Sallies

1951
Battle Creek Belles
Fort Wayne Daisies
Grand Rapids Chicks
Kalamazoo Lassies
Kenosha Comets
Peoria Redwings
Rockford Peaches
South Bend Blue Sox

1952
All Star Team
Battle Creek Belles
Ft. Wayne Daisies
Grand Rapids Chicks
Kalamazoo Lassies
Peoria Redwings
Rockford Peaches
South Bend Blue Sox

1953
Ft Wayne Daisies
Grand Rapids Chicks
Kalamazoo Lassies
Muskegon Belles
Rockford Peaches
South Bend Blue Sox

1954
All Star Team
Fort Wayne Daisies
Grand Rapids Chicks
Kalamazoo Lassies
Rockford Peaches
South Bend Blue Sox

World Series Champions

The first World Series was played in 1903. In the years since, the Series has been played every fall except in 1904 (when the Giants refused to play the A.L. champs), and 1994 (when a labor dispute ended the season in August).

■ *Brad Lidge of the Phillies celebrates a 2008 World Series title.*

Year	Champion
2008	Philadelphia Phillies
2007	Boston Red Sox
2006	St. Louis Cardinals
2005	Chicago White Sox
2004	Boston Red Sox
2003	Florida Marlins
2002	Anaheim Angels
2001	Arizona Diamondbacks
2000	New York Yankees
1999	New York Yankees
1998	New York Yankees
1997	Florida Marlins
1996	New York Yankees
1995	Atlanta Braves
1994	No Series
1993	Toronto Blue Jays
1992	Toronto Blue Jays
1991	Minnesota Twins
1990	Cincinnati Reds
1989	Oakland Athletics
1988	Los Angeles Dodgers
1987	Minnesota Twins
1986	New York Mets
1985	Kansas City Royals
1984	Detroit Tigers
1983	Baltimore Orioles
1982	St. Louis Cardinals

1981	Los Angeles Dodgers	1954	New York Giants	1927	New York Yankees
1980	Philadelphia Phillies	1953	New York Yankees	1926	St. Louis Cardinals
1979	Pittsburgh Pirates	1952	New York Yankees	1925	Pittsburgh Pirates
1978	New York Yankees	1951	New York Yankees	1924	Washington Senators
1977	New York Yankees	1950	New York Yankees	1923	New York Yankees
1976	Cincinnati Reds	1949	New York Yankees	1922	New York Giants
1975	Cincinnati Reds	1948	Cleveland Indians	1921	New York Giants
1974	Oakland Athletics	1947	New York Yankees	1920	Cleveland Indians
1973	Oakland Athletics	1946	St. Louis Cardinals	1919	Cincinnati Reds
1972	Oakland Athletics	1945	Detroit Tigers	1918	Boston Red Sox
1971	Pittsburgh Pirates	1944	St. Louis Cardinals	1917	Chicago White Sox
1970	Baltimore Orioles	1943	New York Yankees	1916	Boston Red Sox
1969	New York Mets	1942	St. Louis Cardinals	1915	Boston Red Sox
1968	Detroit Tigers	1941	New York Yankees	1914	Boston Braves
1967	St. Louis Cardinals	1940	Cincinnati Reds	1913	Philadelphia Athletics
1966	Baltimore Orioles	1939	New York Yankees	1912	Boston Red Sox
1965	Los Angeles Dodgers	1938	New York Yankees	1911	Philadelphia Athletics
1964	St. Louis Cardinals	1937	New York Yankees	1910	Philadelphia Athletics
1963	Los Angeles Dodgers	1936	New York Yankees	1909	Pittsburgh Pirates
1962	New York Yankees	1935	Detroit Tigers	1908	Chicago Cubs
1961	New York Yankees	1934	St. Louis Cardinals	1907	Chicago Cubs
1960	Pittsburgh Pirates	1933	New York Giants	1906	Chicago White Sox
1959	Los Angeles Dodgers	1932	New York Yankees	1905	New York Giants
1958	New York Yankees	1931	St. Louis Cardinals	1904	No Series
1957	Milwaukee Braves	1930	Philadelphia Athletics	1903	Boston Americans*
1956	New York Yankees	1929	Philadelphia Athletics		*later known as the Red Sox
1955	Brooklyn Dodgers	1928	New York Yankees		

*Read the index this way: "**4**:62" means Volume 4, page 62.*

Major League Baseball

Here's an easy way to find your favorite teams in the volumes of this encyclopedia. The numbers after each team's name below indicate the volume and page on which the information can be found. For instance, 1:14 means Volume 1, page 14.

American League

East Division		Central Division		West Division	
Baltimore Orioles	1:24	Chicago White Sox	1:62	Los Angeles Angels of Anaheim	3:26
Boston Red Sox	1:42	Cleveland Indians	1:68	Oakland Athletics	3:80
New York Yankees	3:68	Detroit Tigers	2:8	Seattle Mariners	4:52
Tampa Bay Rays	5:6	Kansas City Royals	3:14	Texas Rangers	5:10
Toronto Blue Jays	5:16	Minnesota Twins	3:50		

National League

East Division		Central Division		West Division	
Atlanta Braves	1:18	Chicago Cubs	1:60	Arizona Diamondbacks	1:14
Florida Marlins	2:36	Cincinnati Reds	1:64	Colorado Rockies	1:74
New York Mets	3:66	Houston Astros	2:72	Los Angeles Dodgers	3:28
Philadelphia Phillies	4:8	Milwaukee Brewers	3:48	San Diego Padres	4:40
Washington Nationals	5:30	Pittsburgh Pirates	4:14	San Francisco Giants	4:42
		St. Louis Cardinals	4:38		

About the Authors

James Buckley, Jr. is the author of more than 60 books for young readers on a wide variety of topics–but baseball is his favorite thing to write about. His books include *Eyewitness Baseball, The Visual Dictionary of Baseball, Obsessed with Baseball,* and biographies of top baseball players, including Lou Gehrig. Formerly with *Sports Illustrated* and NFL Publishing, James is the president of Shoreline Publishing Group, which produced these volumes. Favorite team: Boston Red Sox.

Ted Keith was a writer for *Sports Illustrated Kids* magazine and has written several sports biographies for young readers. Favorite team: New York Yankees.

David Fischer's work on sports has appeared in many national publications, including *The New York Times, Sports Illustrated,* and *Sports Illustrated Kids.* His books include *Sports of the Times* and *Greatest Sports Rivalries.* Favorite team: New York Yankees

Jim Gigliotti was a senior editor at NFL Publishing (but he really liked baseball better!). He has written several books for young readers on sports, and formerly worked for the Los Angeles Dodgers. Favorite team: San Francisco Giants.